FAIRHOPE PU

047

D0935252

FIC   47784
BRO Brown, Virginia Pounds
    Cochula's journey

WITHDRAWN
18.00 Fairhope Public Library

COCHULA'S JOURNEY

ALSO BY VIRGINIA POUNDS BROWN

The Gold Disc of Coosa
Grand Old Days of Birmingham Golf

(Co-Author)
Alabama Mounds to Missiles
Alabama Heritage
Toting the Lead Row: Ruby Pickens Tartt,
Alabama Folklorist
The World of the Southern Indians
Southern Indian Myths and Legends
Winnataska Remembered

(Editor)
Mary Gordon Duffee's Sketches of Alabama

Shell gorget (pendant) with spider design, opposite page, was found in a southeastern prehistoric mound. The gorget worn by Cochula may have looked like this.

7C
RO

COCHULA'S JOURNEY

VIRGINIA POUNDS BROWN

O47784

Black Belt Press

Montgomery

FAIRHOPE PUBLIC LIBRARY
161 N. SECTION ST.
FAIRHOPE, AL 36532

BLACK BELT PRESS
P.O. Box 551
Montgomery, AL 36101

Copyright © 1996 by Virginia Pounds Brown.
All Rights Reserved under International and Pan-American
Copyright conventions. Published in the United States by Black Belt
Press, a division of the Black Belt Communications Group, Inc.,
Montgomery, Alabama.

Book design by Randall Williams

Library of Congress Cataloguing-in-Publication Data
    Brown, Virginia Pounds.
        Cochula's journey / Virginia Pounds Brown
            p. cm.
        Summary: Describes the 1540 De Soto expedition from the
    point of view of the daughter of an Alabama Indian chief whose
    village and people were devastated by the marauding Spaniards.
        ISBN 1-881320-40-5 (hardcover : alk. paper)
        [1. Southern States—Discovery and exploration—Spanish—
    Fiction. 2. De Soto, Hernando, ca. 1500-1542—Fiction. 3.
    America—Discovery and exploration—Spanish—Fiction. 4.
    Indians of North America—Fiction.] I. Title.
    PZ7.B8193Co 1995
    [Fic]—dc20   95-35976
                                                      CIP
                                                       AC

 The Black Belt, defined by its dark, rich soil, stretches across central Alabama. It was the heart of the cotton belt. It was and is a place of great beauty, of extreme wealth and grinding poverty, of pain and joy. Here we take our stand, listening to the past, looking to the future.

For Laurella Owens
who took my penciled scribblings
and performed miracles

Contents

AUTHOR'S NOTE

This book is a work of fiction based on an actual event—De Soto's expedition of 1539–1543 through what is now the southern United States.

We know about that expedition because Spaniards wrote about it. Dates and place names used in this book are historically correct. De Soto, of course, is a historical figure. Cochula is fictional, even though we know in a roundabout way that such a person did exist. All other characters are fictional.

The Journey

The exact route that De Soto and his entourage followed through what is now the southern United States in 1539–1543 is still being debated and investigated. This map is based on the "Swanton route" (1939). A later investigation by the Alabama De Soto Commission (1989) shows a slightly different route.

Courtesy Alabama Department of Archives and History

THE
ROUTE
OF THE
EXPEDITION
OF
HERNANDO DE SOTO
THROUGH THE
SOUTHERN STATES
1539–1543

From the accounts of
Luys Hernandez de Biedma;
the Gentleman of Elvas;
Rodrigo Ranjel;
and Garcilaso de la Vega

Spanish Archives-Sevilla
French Archives-Paris

Reports of B.A.E
Annual report of the
Chief of Engineers U.S.A.
Maps of U.S.G.S
And field investigations of
JOHN R. SWANTON
JAMES Y BRAME
JOHN R. FORDYCE

REVISED 1934

PART I

Coosa to Maubila

July to November 1540

CHAPTER 1

The year was 1540.

The midday sun blazed hot in the Indian town of Coosa. Native people thronged the plaza, anxiously waiting to learn why they had been summoned. Two days ago Spanish forces had occupied Coosa.

"Do nothing more to anger these bearded strangers." Talemicco, chief of Coosa, spoke sharply to Cochula, his daughter, standing by him on a low mound in the plaza. Cochula did not reply. She tossed her head defiantly, and the hawk feather in her headband quivered.

She knew the reason for her father's warning. As they had entered the plaza earlier, a Spanish soldier tried to pull her shawl away from her shoulders. She had turned on him angrily, but Talemicco restrained her; the soldier laughed and pointed his pike threateningly at them as they hurried on.

Sometimes Talemicco wondered where Cochula had come from. She was tall for a young woman of Coosa. And she carried herself with a proud air. Her grandmother, Poosaneeka, said she was like her grandfather. "He came from a people of the north. These people are long-limbed and haughty." Cochula's full cheeks and mouth and her dark, wide, oval eyes, however, marked her as belonging to the people of Coosa. Her skin was tawny colored and smooth, and her shiny black hair fell to her waist. Talemicco called Cochula "My-Little-Tall-One-with-the-High-Head." Her free-spirited ways and her beauty pleased him.

But on this day, with Coosa in peril, Talemicco wanted no trouble from his daughter. He touched the gold disc gleaming on his bare chest in the midday sun, reminding Cochula that he was the chief and was to be obeyed.

Cochula felt anger at her father, and she took it out on her brother, Utina, who sat on the other side of Talemicco.

"Sit tall." Cochula leaned behind Talemicco to pull Utina up by his bear-claw necklace. Utina scowled, but he sat straighter, pushing up the armbands that kept sliding down his thin arms. He flexed his arm muscles to hold up the bands and tried to look older than his age.

He fools no one, Cochula thought. Utina had been born in the full moon of the rabbit fourteen summers ago. She herself had been born sixteen summers ago in the new moon of the green corn, a more propitious time to be born. It was that time now in Coosa.

The sound of heavy boot steps brought Cochula's attention back to the plaza. She saw, striding through the crowd, the heavily armed figure of the Spanish leader, De Soto, his peaked helmet gleaming in the sun. He stopped at the small mound and bowed to Talemicco.

"You are wise to assemble your people as I ordered."

Talemicco bowed in return, the gold disc swinging from his chest. "You are our honored guest and we wish to please you."

De Soto fixed his gaze on the gold disc. He

leaned toward Talemicco to get a closer view but the sun reflecting off the bright metal almost blinded him. He blinked and stepped back. All Coosa knew the bearded strangers sought gold. What would Talemicco do now, Cochula wondered as she watched her father.

Talemicco lifted the disc from his chest, resting it in his hand, and spoke calmly to De Soto. "My ancestors brought the disc from a land far to the west where there is gold. It is always worn by the chiefs of Coosa. Would the Great Leader like to examine it?"

Talemicco seemed about to remove the disc from his neck. But De Soto shook his head.

"In due time," he said with a laugh.

De Soto turned to look at Cochula and then at Utina. "The royal family," he said with a mocking smile. And he bowed again.

Cochula wore her finest deerskin dress, decorated with rows of pearls around the neck and on the fringes.

"The princess of Coosa must have a storehouse of pearls." De Soto stepped up on the mound and came closer to Cochula. He was so close she could see beads of sweat rolling down his swarthy face into his beard. The Spaniard's dark eyes seemed to bore into her. Chills of fear ran over her body.

She wanted to turn and run. But she was Cochula of Coosa, daughter of Talemicco, granddaughter of Poosaneeka. She lifted her head proudly and looked past the Spaniard to the distant mountains. The hot wind blew her hair away from her face.

"Your daughter is like the Indian princess we met at Cofitacheque," said De Soto. "Proud and defiant." He paused. "We now have her pearls in our possession." He turned away with a shrug and strode toward the temple mound.

Cochula felt weak after her close encounter with De Soto. She gripped Talemicco's arm to steady herself.

De Soto climbed halfway up the temple mound and faced the plaza. He pursed his lips and whistled shrilly. Instantly a young Spaniard came through the gate, pulled along by two dogs straining at their leads. Cochula gasped at the sight of them. Were these the dreaded attack dogs, trained to chase Indians and destroy them? The people of Coosa had heard about these animals long before the Spanish army reached Coosa. But they were not prepared for the sight of the giant dogs, so different from the small, almost hairless Indian dogs.

The young Spaniard stopped in front of the low mound, the dogs panting heavily, still on the leash.

Cochula could see the dogs were of two different breeds, one with a thick powerful body, the other slim with long legs. And the youth appeared very different from the other Spaniards. His eyes were blue; Cochula had never seen blue eyes before. His hair was blond, the color of corn tassels, and he had no beard like the other Spaniards.

"Send the mastiff Buteo," De Soto shouted. The youth unchained the shorter, more foreboding-looking dog.

De Soto whistled again and Buteo raced toward him, his thick, reddish coat rolling on his back. The dog sprang up the steps to De Soto, almost knocking him down, his tail wagging furiously in greeting. De

Soto stroked the dog's head. "Down, Buteo," he said.

"Unleash Pepita," De Soto now commanded the youth.

The other dog loped in great strides toward the temple mound but stopped short of De Soto. She sat on her haunches at the foot of the temple mound and looked at De Soto proudly down her long, pointed muzzle.

"The greyhound runs as fast as a snake strikes," De Soto said, adjusting his helmet which Buteo had knocked askew.

Cochula thought Pepita was the most beautiful animal she had ever seen. Surely she was not one of the creatures that killed Indians.

De Soto signaled to a soldier at the back of the plaza, who released one of the Indian slaves the Spaniards had brought to Coosa. The Indian, finding the iron collar gone from his neck, dashed for the open gate.

"Tomaro!" (Attack!) De Soto commanded the dogs. Buteo sprang forward and before the Indian reached the gate knocked him to the ground with his

great paws. Pepita barked but did not charge. As Buteo seemed about to sink his teeth into the man's body, the dog raised his head, then ran back—not to De Soto, but to the youth who stood at the base of the mound.

Cochula could not be sure, but she thought the Spanish youth had recalled the attacking dog in some secret way. De Soto seemed surprised that the dog had returned to the youth.

The two dogs now sat protectively on either side of the youth, watching De Soto. The Spanish leader climbed a few steps higher before he turned to address the people in the plaza. His words struck terror into Cochula's heart.

"Buteo likes the taste of Indian meat. Do not try to run away."

Cochula was afraid for her father, for the people of Coosa, for herself. Talemicco was right to seek peace with these bearded strangers.

That night Cochula lay awake in the chief's house. She could hear the slow, pacing steps of Spanish sentries guarding the house. She could not stop thinking about the beautiful dog Pepita and the blue-eyed youth. Had he saved the Indian's life? Was he different from De Soto and his captains who rode about on their horses, knocking people out of the way?

Just as she was about to sleep, she heard a whispered voice. Talemicco was bending over her. "You are not safe here. Go to the house of your grandmother, Poosaneeka. She will hide you."

From that time the Spaniards made no more pretense of friendliness. Talemicco was run through with a lance when he tried to protect the priests on the temple mound. His body lay on the royal litter in the plaza so the people could see what happened when De Soto was defied. In a mock show, De Soto placed Talemicco's royal cloak around Utina and declared that Talemicco's son was now the chief. He kept

Utina close to his side, holding him hostage.

Cochula hid in her grandmother's house as Talemicco had ordered, disappearing into the corn-crib when soldiers came near. When Poosaneeka told her of Talemicco's death, Cochula's eyes blazed with hatred of the Spaniards, but slowly the fire died. She sat hunched and would not eat. Poosaneeka tended her, singing medicine chants to her. She prepared a ginseng tea, but Cochula would not swallow it.

One day when a soldier came close to Poosaneeka's house, Cochula refused to hide. "Let him find me," she said. But Poosaneeka pushed her in among the dried corn and latched the door until the soldier passed. Later she said, picking corn shucks out of Cochula's hair, "You are the daughter of the chief, the granddaughter of the medicine woman of Coosa. You come from the red earth of Coosa. Get up."

Twenty-four days after the Spaniards had entered the town of Coosa, De Soto was ready to resume his search for gold. The army was rested and well fed.

"Our future lies to the west," De Soto told the captains. "Talemicco promised we would find gold at Maubila."

Accompanied by Father Segura, De Soto's priest who spoke the Indian language, Captain Valdez led a house-to-house search for able-bodied Indians to carry the army's supplies. When the Spaniards neared her house, Poosaneeka forced Cochula into the corn-crib.

As Valdez shouted from his horse for the occupants to come out, Poosaneeka pulled her shawl around her and stepped outside. Through the slats of the crib Cochula could see Poosaneeka standing proudly in spite of her short stature.

"She is old and fat." A soldier prodded Poosaneeka with his pike. Father Segura moved to help her, but she stepped back and lifted her head defiantly.

The soldier prodded her again, this time harder. She lost her balance and fell backwards. Cochula saw Valdez's horse rear and about to come down on her grandmother. Cochula came to life. She flew from her hiding place, pushing aside startled soldiers and

FAIRHOPE PUBLIC LIBRARY

throwing herself over Poosaneeka.

Valdez reined his horse away. "What do we have here?" he said angrily.

Cochula buried her face deeper in her shawl, hoping Valdez would not recognize her.

"Stand her up," he commanded.

A soldier seized Cochula under the arms and held her upright. Poosaneeka steadied herself but remained sitting on the ground, her legs folded under her.

"So this is where the Princess Cochula was hiding. De Soto has been looking for you." Valdez saw the cornhusks clinging to her skirt and caught in her hair. "In a corncrib." He laughed.

"Put her in chains."

Cochula strained to free herself of the guard's grip, biting at the hands grasping her arm. Her hair flew around her face as she struggled, kicking wildly at her captor.

"What shall we do with the old one?" a soldier shouted above Cochula's cries.

"Leave her."

At these words, Poosaneeka stood up and bowed to Valdez. She spoke in a quiet voice to Father Segura. "Tell the honored captain, Cochula spits fire but she will be a good carrier. She is strong and tall with long legs that can walk many miles."

"What is the old woman saying?" Valdez reined his horse impatiently.

Cochula had stopped struggling and was listening to her grandmother. She is up to something, she thought.

Father Segura looked up at Valdez. "She says, the young women of Coosa must learn how to serve you. If you take her with you the old woman will see that they serve you. You will not need chains."

Valdez looked down at the squat figure of Poosaneeka. He recalled the slave women from Ocali who dropped like leaves on the path when they were unable to walk further. Chains had worn ankle bones bare. If gold lay at Maubila, Valdez reasoned, De Soto would want carriers to move fast, without chains.

"Ask her if she has seen the attack dogs," Valdez said to Father Segura.

"She says they know the dogs. They will not try to escape."

"Free the girl." Valdez turned to Poosaneeka. "Have Cochula and fifty more ready to move at daybreak."

Cochula heard her grandmother's grunt of relief as the Spanish soldiers moved away. But Poosaneeka's hands trembled when she pointed for Cochula to enter the house.

"Be quick. We must take all the medicines we can hide."

On August 20, 1540, Cochula's journey began as a captive of the De Soto expedition. At daybreak she fell in line with the other carriers, natives of Coosa, warriors and women alike.

Cochula still wore her deerskin dress, tattered and dirty. Poosaneeka had cut the pearls off and hidden them. But Poosaneeka had found for her a sturdy pair of moccasins. Cochula lifted her reed basket filled with ground corn and slung it onto her back. The rope straps cut into her shoulders, but a headband eased the weight if she leaned forward and tucked her chin as she walked.

"You are not so tall now." Poosaneeka stepped in line beside her granddaughter, nudging her gently in affection. Cochula saw that Poosaneeka had pulled her dark hair streaked with white from her face and plaited it into a neat bun high on her head. Her strong broad face, shining in the morning light, made Cochula's burden feel lighter.

Cochula shifted her pack so she could look at her grandmother.

"And you, Grandmother, are fat as a giant toad." Cochula knew Poosaneeka had stuffed dried herbs and plants in her clothing. Even ginseng was braided into her hair. And somewhere under her flowing skirt was her most sacred possession, her medicine pouch.

CHAPTER 2

De Soto pushed the expedition relentlessly toward Maubila, sure he would at last find gold. Poosaneeka grumbled at the pace, telling Father Segura the packs were becoming too heavy for the women. Poosaneeka herself carried only a light pack, so she could help if a carrier stumbled. At night she gathered sticks and made a little fire for the women to warm aching bodies and keep mosquitoes away. When she tried to tell stories of her people's past, she fell asleep talking.

On most nights, when Cochula eased the pack off her back, she fell to the ground and slept. But sometimes, after Poosaneeka had patted soothing balm to her shoulders, sore from the heavy straps, she lay awake imagining she heard her father's voice singing to her in the pine trees. "My-Little-Tall-One-with-the-High-Head." That was her secret name.

The women were guarded at night by a crippled Spaniard, Ramos, and a giant mastiff named Jabato. Ramos had once been a lancer with the army, but now he nursed a game leg. An Indian at Appalachee had sent an arrow into it. Ramos's temper flared easily and he delighted in teasing the dog. Many times at night on the journey from Coosa, Cochula saw Ramos pop the rawhide whip at Jabato, taunting the dog as he lay chained to a tree.

"Jabato, Jabato. Come get me." At Ramos's words, Jabato would lift his great jowls, baring his teeth, and snarl. As Ramos continued to torment the dog, Jabato would strain at his chains.

Cochula suspected that Ramos was afraid of the dog. And sometimes she was afraid of Ramos. When he narrowed his eyes and smiled at her, showing his white teeth in a black beard, she looked the other way. Poosaneeka had told Captain Valdez that if the Spaniards molested the women of Coosa, the packs they carried would be emptied and their contents stomped on. "When you reach Maubila, you will have nothing," she said. But Cochula could not be sure about Ramos. She spread her mat at night close to her grandmother. Sometimes she rolled over and pressed her back against Poosaneeka's; she did not feel afraid then.

Perhaps her people could find the beloved path again, the path Poosaneeka told about in her stories, that led her ancestors to Coosa and to peace. She would ask Poosaneeka to tell that story some night, and she would stay awake.

Cochula had only glimpsed her brother Utina at a distance since leaving Coosa. One time she saw him being carried on a litter wearing Talemicco's royal cloak as De Soto approached an Indian town. She hoped the Spaniards would do him no harm. She hoped even more he was being brave, remembering to sit tall and keep his armbands up. She longed to see him closer, but there was no way. He was at the head of the force, she at the rear.

De Soto's march to Maubila followed Indian trails leading from one town to another. In each town

De Soto took food, clothing, and a fresh supply of carriers. Not until he reached the province of Taskaloosa did the pattern change. At last the Indians made a stand.

The giant chief, Taskaloosa, greeted De Soto with the usual, hospitable ceremony. He promised to lead the Spaniards to Maubila where, he assured them, they would find gold as Talemicco had promised. Instead, Taskaloosa led De Soto into a trap.

After De Soto and his captains had entered the walled town of Maubila and were resting in the plaza, warriors hiding in the houses swarmed onto the plaza and attacked the unsuspecting Spaniards. De Soto, wounded, managed with the help of one of his captains to escape.

Once outside the gate of the town, De Soto quickly rallied his forces. He and the captains swept back into the town on their horses, brandishing swords and lances. Foot soldiers followed with pikes and guns. Indians—warriors and women alike—fought desperately with clubs, spears, and arrows from house to house. The battle raged all day. For a time it seemed the smoldering fury of the Indians, unleashed at last, would defeat the Spaniards. But when the horsemen tossed lighted torches onto the thatched roofs, Maubila became a flaming inferno.

Thousands of Indians had gathered at Maubila, determined to turn back the Spanish invaders. Most died in the attempt. Many burned to death in the houses; others jumped from the wall or hanged themselves to avoid Spanish captivity. Many of the Spaniards were wounded; forty died. They also lost horses and the pearls from Cofitacheque.

In the woods near Maubila, Cochula and the other slaves heard the raging battle. Their only guard was the game-legged Ramos and the dog Jabato. Cochula knew that Utina had entered the town with De Soto. What was her brother's fate now? She must find a way to help him.

About noonday she heard the thundering charge of the horses into the town, and the cry of the horsemen as they entered the gates. The sound of battle grew even louder as the Indians repulsed the foot soldiers trying to climb the walls.

With a cry, "I must find Utina," Cochula broke away from Poosaneeka and darted out of the woods toward Maubila.

A lance across her body blocked her way. "Where are you going, Princess?"

It was Ramos, the dog panting at his side. Cochula looked at Ramos and quickly stepped back into the trees. Ramos laughed and limped back to sit on a tree stump, picking his teeth with a sweet gum twig.

Cochula did not try to escape again until the night sky turned red as Maubila burned. This time Poosaneeka did not try to stop her. "The night will shelter your way," she said. Cochula took a corn cake from the folds of her skirt and approached the dog. She had been making friends with Jabato, giving him bits of her own food since they left Coosa. Jabato lay at the end of his chain as far from Ramos as he could get, his head resting on his paws, small black eyes almost closed. He watched Cochula as she came nearer.

When Ramos went to the edge of the woods to get a better view of the burning town, Cochula moved even nearer to the dog. Ramos ventured further away, sure Jabato would alert him if Cochula or any other captive tried to escape.

Dropping on her hands and knees, Cochula crept closer toward the chained dog, whispering his name and offering the corn cake. Jabato raised his ears, alert, and sniffed. Cochula had not been this close to the dog before. His wrinkled muzzle looked fierce. She must unfasten the chain from his collar. Fear left her as Jabato lifted his paw and put it on her outstretched arm. He gulped down the food and his tail thumped the ground. She knew now that Jabato would let her pass, but she must stop Ramos from pursuing her.

"Jabato, I am going to free you." Cochula worked to open the catch on the collar.

"Ramos is returning." Poosaneeka hissed a warning. Just as Cochula heard Ramos's step, the catch came loose and the chain fell to the ground, freeing Jabato. Cochula darted past Ramos before he could lift his lance.

With long strides she ran toward Maubila. Behind her she heard Ramos's cries for help when Jabato discovered he was no longer chained and turned on his tormentor.

CHAPTER 3

Cochula crawled through the trampled cornfield to Maubila. She did not want to be spotted by Spaniards fleeing from the burning town. Horses without riders, manes streaming, thundered past her away from the fire. She crawled on, determined to find her brother. When she saw the walls of Maubila, she stood up and ran for the open gate. She dodged past Spanish soldiers fleeing the inferno.

Once inside the gate, she heard cries from the houses. Indians were trapped inside by burning timbers and crumbling walls. Cochula pulled her shawl close around her face to protect herself from the heat of the fire; her eyes streamed tears. Smoke burned her nose and throat, and she gasped for breath.

She wanted to turn and run from the fire as the Spaniards had, but somewhere inside the walls was Utina, and she must find him.

Crouching low, Cochula darted between burning houses and approached the plaza. Busy with their own wounded, the Spaniards paid no heed to the crouched figure of Cochula crawling among the Indian dead and wounded, calling softly, "Utina, Utina."

Cochula did not find Utina. Father Segura had saved him from a Spanish lancer as Utina lay unconscious in the plaza and had taken him to the Spanish camp.

It was Father Segura who, returning to Maubila in the early morning hours, found Cochula, pressed against the earthen steps of the temple mound, blackened with soot and smoke, scarcely able to speak. He knelt by Cochula. She remembered him as the priest who had been kind to Poosaneeka. "I cannot find my brother, Utina," she whispered.

"Utina is safe. De Soto has set him free to return to Coosa." Father Segura spoke softly.

Cochula looked up at the priest. "What of the warriors of Coosa?"

Father Segura glanced about the plaza, littered with fallen bodies. "God have mercy on us," he said.

"The warriors of Coosa are dead. The Spaniards have lost many men and horses. Even our sacred objects are burned."

Cochula drew her shawl closer around her face. She sat with head lowered, not looking at the bloodied plaza. Suddenly she raised her head, listening. Far away, above the crack of falling timbers, she heard a drumbeat. Was Utina sending a message? Cochula stood up, her head high. "The women of Coosa wait for news of the battle. I return to the woods."

She is a fitting daughter for the cacique (chief) of Coosa, thought Father Segura. He put his hand on her arm. "Cochula, help De Soto. He freed your brother."

But a Spanish lance killed my father, she thought.

"What do I have to offer your mighty leader?" Her voice rang with scorn.

"Our wounded need medicine and nursing. We hear there is a medicine woman among you."

"My grandmother, Poosaneeka, is a medicine woman. If we treat your wounded, will De Soto free us?"

"Come," Father Segura said. "I will take you to De Soto. He will answer you."

Cochula followed Father Segura out of the smoldering town to a tent in the Spanish camp where De Soto lay propped on a mat, turned to one side to keep his weight off his wounded hip. His servants surrounded him, viewing his wound. Cochula saw that the arrow which pierced his hip had broken at the skin. She suspected that a stone point lay embedded in the flesh. De Soto writhed in pain, urging his servants to bring him the painkilling drink. When they told him the drink had been lost in the battle, he roared his anger and fell to his side on the mat, groaning.

Father Segura leaned over De Soto. "Sire?"

De Soto raised his head to look at the priest. "Go away, priest. I am not ready to die."

"I have not come for that purpose, Sire. With me is Cochula, daughter of the cacique of Coosa, who would speak with you. She says the women of Coosa have medicines with which to treat our wounds." De Soto turned his head and looked at Cochula.

"Speak," he said.

Cochula could not believe that the dirty, ravaged man lying before her was the proud Spanish leader who had slain her father. She looked down at him. "The women of Coosa wait in the forest for word of the battle. I will tell them the warriors of Coosa lie dead in Maubila. I will tell them the mighty bearded men have need of them. They will come, but only if I tell them they will be free to return to Coosa."

"Tell them that," De Soto gasped, breathing heavily, "and tell them if they try to escape I will send the dogs after them."

"When will we be freed?" Cochula pressed De Soto.

"When we reach the Great River beyond which Utina says lies gold."

De Soto waved Father Segura and Cochula away and called for his surgeon to open his wound and remove the point.

Father Segura took a cross on a chain from his cassock and put it around Cochula's neck. "This will protect you," he said. "Bring the medicine woman."

Cochula left De Soto's tent with the cross clutched in her hand. When a Spanish guard challenged her, blocking her way with his long pike, she lifted the cross in front of her face. The guard lowered the pike and she ran toward the woods.

The sun had crested the mountain, but no rays penetrated the gray haze from the fires. Outside Maubila, Cochula could see groups of Spanish soldiers huddled together, some lying, some sitting. She heard the low moans of the wounded, sharp commands of the captains, and the high-pitched neighings of the horses as they sought to free themselves of their tethers. She covered her nose and mouth against the stench of burning flesh.

As she looked about for a way to get to the woods, she felt a hand grasp her ankle. She recoiled in fear, pulling her foot away. She looked down into the face of a Spaniard, feebly raising his head for help. In the smoke-blackened face Cochula recognized the blue eyes of the youth who had brought the dogs into the plaza at Coosa. Lying at his feet was the dog Buteo, whimpering.

This Spaniard was not like the others, Cochula thought. At Coosa she was convinced he had called the dog off. Pulling the scarf from her head, she knelt by the youth and wrapped the scarf tightly around the bleeding wound on his leg. He moaned at her touch. She rose and raced across the field to the woods.

Cochula could see Poosaneeka with the other women waiting at the edge of the woods for news of the battle. How could she tell them the warriors of Coosa, all save Utina, had perished in Maubila? Her step slowed. She did not know if her legs would hold her up.

Poosaneeka, seeing Cochula stagger, ran to help her. Cochula dropped to her knees before her grandmother.

"The warriors of Coosa are on their long journey to the night land," she said.

Poosaneeka caught Cochula as she slumped to the ground, her strength gone.

A chorus of moans arose from the women. They

covered their faces with their hands and rocked back and forth. The moans became a chant that grew in volume until it reached the Spaniards. They looked to the woods, wondering about the sound. Were there still Indians alive who could attack them? They knew nothing of the Indian lament for the dead.

Poosaneeka revived Cochula, crushing a mint leaf under her nose. "Breathe deeply," she said.

Cochula sighed and opened her eyes; she felt the blood rushing back to her head. Poosaneeka helped her granddaughter to her feet.

"Grandmother, I also bring a message from the bearded leader that concerns all of us."

"Speak it."

Cochula beckoned to the women to sit in a circle around her. Her voice did not waver. "The bearded conqueror lies wounded, a point from a spear piercing his hip. Others suffer wounds and burns. De Soto says the women of Coosa must tend the wounded."

A chorus of guttural hums, and arms waving in denial, greeted Cochula's words. Cochula raised her hand in a gesture she had seen Poosaneeka use to quiet the women. "If we do not help, and we try to escape, he will loose the dogs on us. If we treat the wounded, he will set us free to return to Coosa when we reach the Great River."

Once again protesting cries arose from the women. Poosaneeka now spoke with the authority belonging to a medicine woman. "We must treat the strangers or die," she said. "Who will be left to bear the children of Coosa if we die? Only the old and feeble were left behind. I am old, but I was brought to keep peace among you."

As was the custom in the women's council of Coosa, the women were allowed to speak. One woman said, "I will be chased by dogs before I tend to a bearded man. We can lose the dogs if we are clever."

"If you escape the dogs," Poosaneeka said, "the captains on their horses will find you."

Poosaneeka waited for others to speak. When they did not, she began emptying the medicine packs and giving instructions. Soon she had the women divided into groups.

"We do not have enough medicine for all. I will

take what we have and go to the wounded. Gather acorns," she said to one group. "Boil them and collect the oily scum. We will dress burns with that."

Poosaneeka instructed another group to find sassafras leaves and boil them for treating infections.

When Cochula and Poosaneeka came out of the woods, followed by other women carrying supplies, the Spaniards let them pass. They had been told there was a medicine woman among the captives. Poosaneeka made her way to De Soto's tent and found him with a raging fever and in pain. Father Segura sat at his side. Without ceremony, Poosaneeka leaned over De Soto and grasped him by his beard, tilted his head back, and blew a powder into his nostrils through a medicine tube. At her action, the servants gathered around De Soto's bed moved to seize Poosaneeka, but Father Segura restrained them.

In a few minutes De Soto stopped his restless tossing and fell into a deep sleep. Poosaneeka then dressed the hip wound, laying a poultice of sassafras on the flesh.

Cochula, remembering the wounded youth and

his burned dog, made her way back to the spot where he had been lying. He was now half-sitting, his leg no longer bleeding, but blisters had appeared on his face. His teeth were bared in pain. She broke the stem of a milkweed plant and touched the burns with the secretion. The youth's grimace disappeared as his pain was relieved.

"Gracias (Thank you)," he murmured, falling back in relief to the ground. Cochula saw that Buteo's left withers had no hair and the skin was burned black.

Until nightfall Poosaneeka and Cochula and the other women of Coosa tended the men of De Soto's force. The women moved quietly, stopping at times to gaze at the smoke still spiraling from the wooden houses of Maubila. They obeyed the orders of the captains. When they returned to the woods for the night, guards with dogs accompanied them. The women of Coosa were as valuable now as the gold De Soto sought.

Ramos, Cochula noted, was not one of the guards. Nor was Jabato among the dogs.

At the camp in the trees Cochula drew her sleeping mat close to her grandmother's. Poosaneeka had wrapped herself in a blanket against the night chill.

"What will we do tomorrow, Grandmother?"

"We will tend to the bearded men and we will live. Our ancestors came the way we are going, from the navel of the earth, many moons ago. They made a little journey each day. First they found fire. Then water. Then their medicine. Then they found Coosa and there they settled down.

"So we will make a little journey each day. Now, sleep."

"But I am afraid, Grandmother."

"You are a medicine woman now," Poosaneeka said. "Medicine women have power from the spirits. And they are never afraid."

Cochula did not believe that her grandmother was never afraid. But she was pleased to hear Poosaneeka call her a medicine woman.

CHAPTER 4

The blue-eyed youth Antonio lay where he had fallen, until the afternoon sun broke at last through the smoke-filled sky and burned his face. He sat up, remembering the wild charge into Maubila with the dogs as they chased the Indians who were running to escape the fires. He remembered being burned and cut and crawling out of the gate with the dog Buteo, who also was burned. He remembered the tall Indian girl bending over him, touching his face.

Antonio reached out, feeling for the dog, his fingers brushing Buteo's hair. Buteo did not respond. Antonio looked down and saw the empty eyes, the still form of the once-powerful mastiff. Sobs racked Antonio's body.

It was thus that Captain Rodriguez, De Soto's next in command, found him. "De Soto will not be pleased to know of Buteo's death," he said.

"The dogs should not have been taken into the burning city," Antonio muttered. But the captain heard him.

"Tell that to De Soto." Rodriguez reined his horse directly over Antonio. "The Adelantado says all wounded horses and dogs are to be done away with—now."

Antonio obeyed the Adelantado's orders about the dogs, with one exception. When he found the greyhound bitch, Pepita, whimpering and licking her burned paws, he picked her up and carried her to the brush enclosure where the dogs were kept. He treated her front feet with fat, muzzled her, and tied her to a tree. He rubbed her neck affectionately, assuring her he would return.

Pepita was a full-blooded Spanish greyhound of aristocratic lineage. She had made the journey from Spain to the New World in Antonio's care. Antonio favored her over the other dogs, and her devotion to him knew no bounds.

At De Soto's suggestion, Pepita had been mated with Buteo. Antonio questioned the crossbreeding of a mastiff and a greyhound, but when he looked at Pepita's fat belly he smiled. Her puppies would be his to train.

In Spain Antonio had helped his father train dogs for the army of King Charles. Royal dogs fought on the battlefield along with the soldiers. Antonio was proud of the dogs of war raised in his father's kennels. But he had become less proud.

The trouble had started when the Cuban dog Buteo came aboard the ship in Havana. Buteo was a mastiff but very different from the Spanish breed that Antonio knew. Buteo had been bred from the attack dogs that Cortez, the earlier Spanish conquistador, used against the Aztecs in Mexico. These dogs had been trained for one purpose: to pursue and attack Indians.

De Soto took a liking to Buteo, and each day while on the ship, he had Antonio bring the dog to him. Buteo quickly had become the leader of the pack, and he did not always respond to Antonio's command. Antonio did not know what to do.

Antonio was beginning to wonder why he had

left his home in Spain. When Captain Rodriguez came to buy dogs for De Soto, Antonio had begged his father to send him to handle the dogs. The boy had dreamed of adventures in the New World and of returning to Spain a rich young man laden with gold.

That dream had died as De Soto's army hacked its way through dense forests and over swollen streams in the land they called Florida. They had found no gold, only Indians. It seemed to Antonio that De Soto had turned to hunting Indians with dogs for the sport of it. That had been true at Ocali.

When the Spanish expedition had reached Ocali soon after coming ashore, the town was empty. The inhabitants had fled to the woods. That night the Spaniards feasted on the corn they found and on fresh fruit and dried fish.

Early the next morning four Indians came out of the woods, wearing feathered headdresses, carrying no weapons, their arms raised in salute. Slowly they approached the town plaza where De Soto sat with the captains, still feasting on the first fresh food they had eaten since leaving Cuba. The dog Buteo lay at

De Soto's feet, waiting to be dropped a morsel.

"Tell them we come in peace," De Soto spoke to a captain. "Tell them to look on the might of Spain. We are a mighty army from across the waters." De Soto pointed to the horses being saddled for the day and at the lancers already dressed in their jackets of mail.

"Ask them if they know of a yellow metal soft enough to bite."

The Indians listened and shook their heads when asked about the gold. Then they pointed to the horses in puzzlement. De Soto commanded one of the captains to mount his horse and ride around the plaza. The captain put his horse through his paces, stopping quickly, turning, galloping. Suddenly the Spaniard charged toward the Indians as if he were going to ride into them, but he brought the horse up just short.

The charge was too much for the Indians, who thought they would be run down. They turned and raced toward the woods.

Buteo, trained to chase fleeing Indians, raced

after them. He attacked the fastest one first, bringing him to the ground with one stroke of a heavy paw. The other three men scattered, but Buteo managed to fell them all. When the dog returned to De Soto's side, feathers from the Indians' headdresses clung to his bloody muzzle.

Later, Indians appeared at the edge of the forest, carrying spears and arrows. They dragged the wounded men to the shelter of the trees.

That night Antonio went to the tent of Father Segura, who heard his confessions. "The dog Buteo attacked the Indians today—and he was not commanded to."

The flame of an oil lamp flickered between the priest and the youth. "Buteo is a Cuban dog," Father Segura said. "He was bred to run down Indians."

"But the four Indians today wanted to talk. The Adelantado should have stopped Buteo."

Father Segura studied the youth. There was only the shadow of a beard on his face. So young and so far from the remote hills of the Estremadura, the priest thought. And so unaware of how lust for gold could poison men's souls. Yet Antonio was right. De Soto should have called the dog back. Indians were not animals to be hunted for sport.

But to Antonio he said, "You care about the dogs?"

Antonio replied, "I am their keeper. They trust me."

"Then do not defy De Soto. He will destroy whatever stands between him and the gold."

After that Antonio began his plan to win Buteo's loyalty. As far as it was possible to do so without De Soto knowing about it, he kept Buteo apart from the other dogs. He brought him into the tent where he slept and chained him to the tent post. He talked to him and brushed his coat each day. He whittled a piece of cane to make a high-pitched whistle that only dogs could hear. His father had used such a whistle in training dogs in Spain. At first Buteo seemed puzzled at the sound, but soon he came running to Antonio, who rewarded the dog with a choice morsel saved from his own scarce fare.

By the time the expedition reached Coosa, Antonio believed Buteo would follow his commands. And so he did. But now, one year after Ocali, Buteo was dead, burned at Maubila.

⚭

The Spanish force rested after the battle of Maubila. Antonio's leg wound healed slowly, and the burns on his face left only small red splotches. Each day Antonio saw Cochula with her grandmother, dispensing medicines, treating wounds. Sometimes he could feel Cochula's eyes on him, and he would say her name softly to himself. He had learned her name from Father Segura.

She is beautiful, Antonio thought, observing Cochula's black hair shining in the sunlight and the proud set of her head. And she is brave to move among her enemies.

Antonio had no doubt that De Soto would cut the noses from the faces of these women captives if they tried to escape. He had seen it done to the Apalachee Indians and others earlier in the expedition.

Soon, he told himself, De Soto will turn back to the sea. We have lost everything, even the pearls from Cofitacheque, all because of this search for gold.

The Spaniards grew more and more restless. Around the campfires at night they talked of how many days' journey it would be to the gulf. "Surely our ships lie there," they said.

Antonio dared to dream of seeing his home in Spain again. Would his family know him with his fair skin tanned like an Indian's or his hair bleached white by the sun? He had the beginnings of a beard and his legs were longer.

One month after the battle of Maubila, De Soto was able to mount his horse, and others of the wounded could travel. The dead had been buried. De Soto addressed the force: "On the morrow we leave this wretched place," he said. "We will make our way to the Great River beyond which our treasure lies. Utina, the cacique of Coosa, has shown me the way." De Soto held up the parchment on which Utina had drawn a map. A murmur of disbelief arose from the men.

He is truly mad, Antonio thought. Does he not know that the Indians always promise gold just beyond their borders? Antonio joined in the cry of protest from the Spaniards. Captain Rodriguez spoke:

"But, Sire, we have no supplies, no medicine, no food. Even our sacred objects are lost."

The Adelantado's voice thundered, "The Indian granaries to the west are full. Would you return to Spain as poor as when you left it?"

CHAPTER 5

While the Spaniards recovered from their wounds, Cochula and her grandmother searched the woods and fields near Maubila for medicine plants. One day Poosaneeka spotted a red willow tree and called to Cochula, "*Miko hoyanidja* (killer of pain)."

Poosaneeka beckoned to their Spanish guard to help dig the root. The guard, under orders to assist Poosaneeka in whatever she needed, leaned his pike against a tree and came to help. As he dug, Cochula and her grandmother pulled at the roots, careful not to break the rootlets.

Cochula remembered that as a child in Coosa she liked to help Poosaneeka, holding the basket as her grandmother filled it with stems, roots, leaves, or even flowers for her medicines. If she found a rare herb or an unusual rock, Grandmother carefully put it aside. Later it might go into a small deerskin pouch.

Cochula had never been allowed to carry this pouch or even to look in it. It was Poosaneeka's sacred bundle.

"Every plant has its purpose," Grandmother would say.

"How do you know that purpose?" Cochula would ask.

"I learned it from my grandmother, and you will learn from me."

Then Poosaneeka added, "If there is a plant we don't know about, the spirit of the plant will tell us."

Cochula knew this was part of a myth that only Poosaneeka as a medicine woman was allowed to tell. Usually Poosaneeka told the myth on special occasions, like the fall corn festival. But when Cochula asked to hear it, Poosaneeka stopped gathering plants and folded her short legs under her and sat down, beckoning Cochula to sit facing her. "This is the story of the animals' revenge," Poosaneeka began in her storytelling voice.

"Once, when the earth was getting overpopulated, the people killed too many animals. The people needed animals for food, but the animals—deer, bear, wolf—feared they would all become extinct. So they decided to strike back.

"They sent all kinds of terrible diseases to plague people. When the plants, who were friendly to people, learned of this plan, they said, 'We will furnish a cure for every disease the animals send.'

"And that's how we got our medicine."

Grandmother always ended her story by opening her arms wide, as if to embrace the earth. "Every tree, shrub and herb, even the grasses and mosses, furnished a cure. Each said, 'I will help man.'"

When Cochula and Poosaneeka would return to town with the plants, the people respectfully stepped aside for the medicine woman of Coosa, who walked sure and straight in spite of her short stature. Cochula was proud to be with her grandmother, helping to hold the overflowing basket of plants.

Now she and Poosaneeka were far away from Coosa. They were slaves, digging roots to treat the wounds of Spanish soldiers. They were under the eyes of a Spanish guard.

As she tugged at the willow root, Poosaneeka stopped several times to scratch her reddened arms. Her face was flushed.

When they had loosened the root, Poosaneeka stood up. She swayed and would have fallen had Cochula not caught her.

"Grandmother, a fire burns in you."

"We will make the red willow tea, and the fire will leave me."

But the fire in Poosaneeka worsened. That night Cochula lay by her grandmother, who suffered terrible aching and fever. Cochula held her to warm her when the chills came.

At daybreak Cochula saw that her grandmother's face and hands were covered with small blisters. "What is it, Grandmother?"

"It is a rash from the mosquito bites. We have no bear grease to protect us."

The next day sores began forming in Poosaneeka's mouth and throat. Her voice weakened. "This is not from mosquitoes. It is a disease for which we have been given no medicine," she told Cochula.

Cochula sent the other women to the Spaniards, but she stayed by her grandmother that day. By nightfall pustules started to form on Poosaneeka's neck and face. Cochula brewed a willow tea, but Poosaneeka could not swallow. She begged Cochula to take her to the stream, to let her sit in the cool water to ease the terrible itching.

"Cleanse me, cleanse me," she said between clenched teeth. "The water will cleanse me."

Cochula, holding her grandmother under her arms, carried her to the stream. The water was cold, but Cochula eased Poosaneeka down until only her face showed. She cupped water in her hand and let it trickle down her grandmother's blotched, swollen face.

"Ah. Ah." As her pain eased, Poosaneeka's eyelids closed and she rested, Cochula supporting her in the water. Suddenly Poosaneeka began coughing, and Cochula hurriedly lifted her out of the stream. Back on her mat, Poosaneeka could not stop shaking and coughing.

Poosaneeka did not die that night, even though

the sores in her mouth and throat blocked her breathing. She rallied once, clutching Cochula's arm in a desperate grasp, pulling her close. She could not speak, but she pulled at the top of the mat where she lay, trying to turn it up. Her strength failed and she fell back, gasping for breath.

She wants something, Cochula thought. She leaned over her grandmother. "Tell me."

Poosaneeka's eyes burned like embers. She made another desperate attempt to raise her head and reach under the mat.

"Her medicine bundle. She has hidden it under the mat." Cochula rolled her grandmother on her side and reached under the mat. Pressed down almost flat was the deerskin pouch.

"I have it, Grandmother." Cochula bent down, holding the bundle close to Poosaneeka's face.

With the last bit of her strength, Poosaneeka pushed the pouch toward Cochula.

Cochula knew her grandmother was passing to her the sacred possession of a medicine woman. She took the pouch and strapped it around her waist under her deerskin dress. This was the way Poosaneeka had brought it safely from Coosa.

∾

The next day half the women of Coosa had fever and could not go to the Spanish camp. Cochula resolved to seek Father Segura's help.

The Spanish camp bustled with activity as the army readied to move again. Cochula found Father Segura preparing a mass for the upcoming journey.

"Poosaneeka is dying," she told him. "And many more are sick. We do not know this sickness. We have no medicine."

Father Segura saw the desperation on Cochula's face. "I will come," he said.

He followed Cochula across the field to the women's enclosure in the trees. When he saw Poosaneeka he fell back with a cry. "Smallpox! It is a scourge," he said. He had seen tribes in Peru wiped out by the disease. "I will tell De Soto."

When De Soto learned that smallpox had broken out among the Coosa women and that the head medicine woman was dying, he cursed Father Segura and urged the captains to hasten the preparations for departure.

Father Segura sought out Antonio to tell him of the smallpox among the Coosa women. "Will we leave them to die?" Antonio asked.

"De Soto says we begin our march tomorrow."

On that same night, the greyhound Pepita gave birth to puppies. Two survived. Antonio prepared a litter in which the pups could be carried until their eyes opened and they were able to follow with the other dogs.

Antonio took a torch and went to the women's camp. He heard no sound, saw no movement. There was no need for dogs or guards now. A putrid odor hung in the air, an odor he remembered in his own village in Spain when smallpox struck. Many had died; he had survived, his mother claimed, because she had not sent him to the pest house but nursed him herself with her special salve and chamomile tea.

Antonio called Cochula's name. A moan answered him. Swinging his torch around, he saw Cochula holding her grandmother, whose body was arched in death. As he moved his torch around the circle, Antonio observed that all the women lay on their mats, their eyes, like fiery beads in their swollen faces, fixed on him. He looked again at Cochula. A rash covered her face. She was singing and rocking Poosaneeka's stiffened body. When she raised her eyes to Antonio, he realized her gaze was sightless. The fever has taken her mind, he thought. She was hot to the touch.

Antonio tried to force Cochula's arms loose from her grandmother's body. One hand would not release the shell gorget around Poosaneeka's neck. Antonio slipped the pendant over the dead woman's head and then over Cochula's, where it hung with the cross given her by Father Segura.

Supporting Cochula, with one of her arms around his neck, Antonio made his way to the encampment. He placed Cochula on the litter with Pepita and the puppies. They would warm her when the chills came.

To grease her sores he would use the salve his mother had made for him. Traveling at the rear of the army with the herd of swine, the litter carried by two dispirited Apalachee Indians who had no noses, Antonio thought they would be safe.

It was now November 14, 1540. Cochula once more journeyed with the De Soto expedition, but this time she was not carrying the Spaniards' supplies on her back. She lay hidden in a litter with the puppies, tended by the Spanish youth Antonio.

Cochula did not know when the expedition left Maubila, but as they neared the chiefdom of the Apafalaya, her eyelids no longer stuck together and she could see that the land was different.

She had stopped fighting Antonio when he treated her sores. And she ate when the dogs ate. She had lost her hair with the fever, and Antonio had covered her head with his own hood.

She remembered that Antonio had tied her hands together when she tried to claw at the sores that tormented her. "You will be pitted like a peach seed if you scratch," he said.

The first day that the newborn pups rode in the litter with Cochula, Pepita trailed the litter nervously. When the litter was lowered, she made a dash for the pups, who tumbled out ready to nurse. On the first night, the puppies curled up next to Cochula, but Pepita, tethered outside, whined so protestingly that Antonio loosed her to sleep with Cochula and the pups.

Cochula awoke one morning, her fever gone, to a gentle but persistent licking of her face. The puppies lay one on each side of her, cleansing first themselves and then her. Their mother Pepita was on a mission with Antonio. Cochula remembered that as her delirium came and went, the warm, furry bodies had pressed against her. She remembered reaching out and pulling the pups to her when they whimpered. Now that they were weaned, they ran alongside the litter or wandered into the underbrush. If Pepita was not there to bring them back, Cochula called them with a clucking of her tongue.

What had happened at Maubila and Coosa had grown dim in her mind. She did not try to recall it. It was as if all that had happened to another person, not to her. She had become part of the Spanish expedition. Now she had no desire to escape. She wanted only to survive.

Just a little journey each day, Grandmother had said. Cochula did remember that. So she made herself eat the wormy corn cakes. She rubbed Antonio's salve into her scaly skin. Sometimes when she fell behind the long line of slaves carrying supplies, the pups came loping back to find her. Cochula stumbled along between them until she caught up.

"The shock of the medicine woman's death and the fever from the smallpox have changed her," Father Segura said to Antonio as they observed Cochula walking listlessly, her eyes sunk far back in her head.

"The dogs will help her get well," Antonio said. "Please do not tell De Soto where she is."

PART II

To Chickasaw Country

November 1540 to April 1541

CHAPTER 6

By early winter, Cochula was stronger and her eyes brighter. She was clad now in a ragged doublet Antonio had taken from a soldier killed at Maubila. She had fashioned a hood-like covering of her own from rabbit skin for her head and shoulders. The Spaniards took her for Antonio's helper, another lad seeking his fortune in the New World, his face pitted from smallpox.

Her hair had grown almost enough to cover her ears, but her skin felt rough as she rubbed grease into it. She had seen her reflection when she bathed in a stream, and she did not look again. Her face was splotched and swollen. She kept the hood pulled close around her face to protect herself from the cold and to hide her face.

Cochula helped herd the swine, prodding the grunting animals with a stick to keep them moving.

When the swine wandered off the path, the pups helped her round them up. Antonio would laugh when he saw the three of them chasing squealing pigs between pine trees.

Antonio had named the pups Pedro and Zia. He chose "Pedro" because of an honored dog of war from his father's kennels. He chose "Zia" because it sounded Indian, and he thought Cochula would like that. Already he sensed a bonding between Cochula and the female pup Zia.

Zia was going to be like her mother, a true greyhound. Pedro, on the other hand, was already stocky like a mastiff, with a short, straight tail and a worried look. Very like Buteo, his sire, Cochula thought. Both dogs had short, thick hair. Zia's coat was becoming mottled, whereas Pedro's was solid tan. And Zia was marked like Pepita, with white muzzle, chest, and feet. Her tail was long and curled elegantly, to the delight of Pedro, who tried in vain to catch it.

De Soto was now desperate to find food and shelter from the winter cold. Scouts reported the rich province of the Chickasaws lay ahead, but a wide river must be crossed to reach it. When they reached the river, De Soto ordered the expedition to make camp. Barges would be built on which to cross.

On the first night of the encampment, Antonio approached the guards outside De Soto's tent, asking to see the Adelantado.

"It is urgent, about the dogs," he said.

The guard beckoned Antonio to enter. De Soto was huddled close to the fire. Antonio swallowed his fear and approached the Adelantado.

"Speak," De Soto said without looking up.

"I beseech you, Sire, to spare food for the dogs. They grow thinner and weaker with each day's journey."

"Let them die." De Soto gazed into the fire, where a pig was roasting.

The smell of the meat almost overwhelmed Antonio; he looked away. The pig was for the captains, not for dog-keepers such as he. He felt weak from hunger and cold but he spoke again.

"But, Sire, these are the dogs of war—noble dogs trained in warfare. We cannot let them die."

"We no longer need dogs to track down Indians. Our slaves will not try to escape in this cold and barren land."

De Soto pulled his padded jacket closer to his body. "We must find a friendly cacique across the river and make winter camp, or we will all die." With a wave of his hand he dismissed Antonio.

Antonio did not leave. "Sire, I request permission to loose the dogs at night so they can hunt for food."

De Soto threw back his head, his beard pointing upward at the heavens, and laughed. "How many would come back, having tasted fresh meat and freedom, my foolish dog-keeper?"

If I lose the dogs, Antonio thought, it will be to the wolves. For many nights he had listened to the wolves' howls. Once he had glimpsed gleaming yellow eyes and a flash of reddish hair passing in the light of the fire. He knew from experience in the mountains of Spain that dogs and wolves were natural enemies.

But to De Soto he said, "I will go with the pack, Sire, and bring them back."

"You think of dogs when gold lies in our reach." De Soto shook his head. "Perhaps the dogs will frighten the Indians lurking on the trail watching us." With a curt nod De Soto gave in to Antonio's request.

"Let the dogs hunt."

The dogs of war wasted no time in finding meat. They tracked down rabbits, opossums, and other small animals. Antonio kept the pack together, except for Jabato.

The wolves sensed their territory had been invaded; they watched and waited. When the wolves howled, Jabato's tail straightened and his ears came forward. One night Jabato ignored Antonio's whistles to return from the hunt to camp. Instead, he followed the scent of the wolves. The dog did not know some of the wolf pack were also tracking him. When he put his muzzle in a rabbit burrow, two wolves attacked his rear.

Jabato turned and ran from the snarling wolves, his ears laid back and his tail between his legs, until he caught up with Antonio and the other dogs.

Later, Cochula examined Jabato's rump and treated it. "The wounds are not deep. He is nipped in several places," she reported to Antonio.

"Wolves?" Antonio questioned.

"Wolves," Cochula answered. "Just a warning. Stay off our mountain."

From that night, Antonio had no more trouble with Jabato obeying his commands.

Early one morning Antonio returned to camp carrying a white-tailed buck across his shoulders. He had gone without the dogs before daybreak to a spot where he had seen deer crossing. Using a bow and arrow, he brought the buck down and finished him off with his spear.

When Cochula saw the deer, she called excitedly

to the captive women nearby. They formed a circle around the animal and bowed to it as they sang.

"We thank the spirit of the deer for this gift," Cochula explained to Antonio.

The Spanish youth watched the women dress the deer. About half of the animal would be eaten by the Spaniards, but the rest would supply the slaves with some of their needs. Antlers and bones would be made into needles, fishhooks, drills, pins. Sinews and guts would make threads for sewing. And the hide, once cured, would make a few moccasins and shirts.

Cochula claimed a sharp rib bone which she would use as a hairpin. Someday her hair would be long again. Later she slipped it into her deerskin pouch.

"You waste nothing." Antonio looked at what remained of the animal. He thought how much the Spaniards would have thrown away.

That night, far back from the main Spanish force, the Indian slaves built a fire and danced around it. Dried deerskin had been stretched over a gourd to make a drum.

"We dance for our brother, the deer, who has given us so much." Cochula folded her hood over her arm and joined the women in a slow, rhythmic step, following the men dancers. For the first time since Maubila and the terrible sickness, she felt alive.

The lead dancer stopped in front of Antonio and bowed to him. "The slayer of the deer will dance." Antonio found himself responding to the incessant beat of the drum and joined the dance.

When Captain Rodriguez, having been sent by De Soto to investigate the drumbeat, saw the dancers and the long-legged Spanish youth in the midst of them, he went back and reported to De Soto.

"They are engaged in a heathen ritual." He suggested they be allowed to continue. "Tomorrow their burdens will be lighter because of the refreshing of their spirits."

"Good." De Soto nodded sleepily at the captain's words.

The captain made no mention of Antonio. When he was a young man serving in Peru, Rodriguez had been fascinated with the Incas. But he resolved to have a word tomorrow with Antonio. It was danger-ous to fraternize with slaves.

Cochula could not forget the sight of Antonio dancing, the white tail of the deer swinging from his waist.

Another night, as the expedition waited for the barges to be built to cross the river, Cochula lay close to the fire, the pups snuggled to her back for warmth. She heard Antonio's step and looked up to see him with the dogs, ready for another hunt. Even in the firelight she could see his wide, blue eyes. She felt warmed by their gaze. But still she pulled the hood closer around her face when he looked at her.

"Guard the swine until I return," Antonio said. "The men in the camp are hungry." With that warn-ing Antonio disappeared into the shadows.

At the campfire, Cochula dozed off, but was awakened by a rustling close to the swine pen. The pups raised their heads, their ears up. Cochula eased the cover from her face. A crouched figure crawled toward the pen. As light from the fire fell on the man, Cochula recognized Ramos. Not only did he have a game leg, but now one arm hung at his side, made useless by the dog's attack at Maubila. In his other hand Ramos held a dagger. He is so hungry he would steal a pig, Cochula thought.

When Ramos stood up and leaned over the low fence to stab a sleeping pig, Pedro growled and lunged at the bent figure. Surprised, Ramos turned, and as the pup leaped on him he thrust the blade into the dog's belly. Pedro fell back. Before Ramos could withdraw his knife, Cochula and Zia sprang on him. Cursing and flinging his good arm, Ramos tried to shake off the dog who had a hold on his leg. Cochula, wild with fury, pounded on Ramos's head.

Sentries nearby heard Ramos's cries and ran to pull apart the three figures rolling on the ground. One sentry held Cochula while the other kicked Pedro until he let go of Ramos's arm. Ramos slowly rose. He looked at Cochula, her black eyes smoldering, her pitted face forgotten. In her anger she had let her hood fall from her face.

"I have seen those eyes before," said the Spaniard. "Call the captain," he said to the sentries. "The

Adelantado will thank me for finding this treacherous wench who has twice tried to kill me."

Ramos thrust his face close to Cochula's. "Once I longed for you, my dark beauty. But who wants a pitted toad?"

With an iron collar on a chain around her neck, Cochula was brought before De Soto. The Adelantado was warming first one side of his body and then the other at the fire. Rain was turning into snow. Cochula shivered.

"Ramos tells me you are not what you seem to be," said the Adelantado. "He tells me you are Cochula, daughter of Talemicco, cacique of Coosa. You are the sister of Utina."

De Soto leaned forward to look closely at Cochula. "The women of Coosa died with smallpox at Maubila. Maybe you did not die." He thrust his face close to Cochula's. In spite of the smallpox scars, he recognized her. "You defied me in the plaza at Coosa. But you came with the medicine woman to treat my wound at Maubila. You are Cochula."

Cochula did not speak.

"Why were you among the swine?"

"Antonio left me to guard them. Ramos was stealing a pig. I stopped him." Cochula made no mention of the pups. Antonio does not want De Soto to know about them, she thought.

"So Ramos lusted for pig meat." De Soto rose and strode around and around Cochula, studying her. Cochula followed him with her eyes.

"Your brother Utina drew me a map—the way to the gold beyond the Great River," said De Soto. "Do you know this way?"

My brother was clever to draw a map of a way he did not know, Cochula thought. Traders from across the Great River brought silver and precious stones to the square at Coosa, but never had she seen gold. Utina must have drawn the map to send De Soto to the setting sun, away from Coosa, Cochula reasoned.

"The way is long, through many chiefdoms," Cochula said to De Soto. "But when you cross the Great River, the path becomes broad to the mountains and the gold."

"Talemicco sent me from Coosa to Maubila

with promises of gold," De Soto replied. "But there was no gold—only Indians eager for our destruction. I think Ramos has done me a great service by finding you."

De Soto spoke sharply to one of his captains. "Free her. A daughter of a cacique must be treated with respect, especially if she is a medicine woman. She will be carried on a litter, just as Utina was, to meet the next cacique. We must find winter quarters.

"But first we must find suitable attire for this Indian princess." De Soto looked scornfully at Cochula's ragged clothing. He was sure that a handsome deerskin dress and shawl lay hidden in one of his captain's chests, probably taken at Apafalaya, the last town the Spaniards occupied. It was bounty to be carried back to Spain, a souvenir from the New World.

De Soto turned to the captain who had brought Cochula to him. "See that Cochula has a dress and shawl suiting her high station.

"Summon Father Segura," De Soto ordered. "Cochula will be in his care."

Antonio returned to camp before dawn. There he found Pedro dead from the wound from Ramos's dagger. On their hunting trip the dogs had feasted on small game. Some of the meat Antonio had brought back. But at the sight of the dead pup, the joy of the chase and the kill vanished. What had happened to Cochula and to Zia?

CHAPTER 7

Cochula lay shivering on her mat in Father Segura's quarters. She missed the warm bodies of the dogs pressed against her. She missed knowing that Antonio was near. She had scorned the blanket Father Segura had given her, leaving it at her feet, but now she drew it around her curled-up body and tried to stop shaking.

"It's a long journey, Grandmother." A shudder ran through her as she remembered Maubila. Did Poosaneeka's bones lie bare, unburied, ravaged by animals? "I will not think about these things," she said.

Instead she listened to the night noises. She heard the Spanish guard just outside stomping his feet and beating his hands together to keep warm. She smelled smoke from the fires the Spaniards kept going all night for warmth and protection. She thought she heard raindrops on the thatched roof, but there was no splattering, only a soft thud. Then she became aware of a faint whimpering. It was Zia. Sitting up, she whispered the dog's name. Zia crawled onto the mat with her. Cochula reached for the dog and found Zia's coat wet with snow. The dog nudged Cochula's hand with her cold nuzzle and Cochula hugged her. Cochula knew Pedro was dead. And Zia, lost without her litter mate, using her inborn tracking skills, had found Cochula in De Soto's quarters.

Cochula no longer shook as she soothed the trembling dog. "Be brave," she said. "Tomorrow I will make you a collar. You are my sister dog." Zia's tail began to thump, and the dog stopped trembling.

"That is your secret name—Sister Dog," Cochula whispered into the pup's ear.

The next morning Captain Rodriguez brought Cochula a finely made deerskin dress and shawl. She wasted no time in discarding her old clothing and donning the dress. The soft feel of the deerskin took her back to Coosa. She hugged Zia, and for the first time since Poosaneeka died, she wept.

Later, remembering her promise to the dog, she gathered scraps of dried deerskin and cut them into narrow pieces. She took bloodroot and black walnuts from her medicine supplies and boiled them separately in pots on a cooking fire. She dyed some of the deerskin pieces red with bloodroot; some she dyed brown with walnuts.

Sitting on her haunches close to the fire, she wove the strips together to make a wide collar. As she worked she talked to Zia. The dog also sat on her haunches, watching Cochula questioningly, turning her head from side to side as Cochula talked.

"You are a royal dog, and this will be a royal collar. I will weave a headband for myself in the same colors. I will put a feather in mine—a hawk's feather, because I am a chief's daughter." Cochula worked her fingers rapidly. "And when we walk through the camp, the captains will bow and they will know you belong to me." Her fingers tied a knot with an angry jerk.

De Soto, passing by to inspect the barges, eyed the pair, Zia with her black and red collar, Cochula with her matching headband and clad in a deerskin dress, but he said nothing. He must cross the river and find winter quarters. He needed Cochula as an emissary and, more importantly, as a medicine woman to his ailing army.

After crossing the river, the Spaniards traveled northwest; this direction would lead to the Great River and to gold. So Utina had told De Soto at Maubila. Cold winds, whipping out of the west, brought more snow. There were no Indian towns to supply food and shelter. Antonio, with the dogs, spent more of each day and night looking for game. No longer did the dogs of war hunt Indians; they hunted game for themselves and for the army.

Finally De Soto summoned a captain and ordered him to ride ahead until he found a friendly cacique.

Three days later the captain returned.

"God is with us," he said to De Soto. "A town lies ahead, its storage bins spilling over with food."

"What of the cacique? Did he greet you?"

"No. Strangely, the town is empty of people."

De Soto gave orders to move at once, in spite of the snow and sleet. Cochula knew the expedition had entered the land of the Chickasaws, a people known as crafty and fierce, enemies of Coosa. Cochula doubted that the countryside was as unoccupied as it seemed.

When the Chickasaw town came into view a day later, De Soto ordered Cochula to be placed on a litter. De Soto and the captains on their horses entered the town first. Cochula, the litter held high, rode behind them. She wore her headdress with the hawk's feather. Zia walked under the carrier, her head and long, curving tail low, her pace as measured as the litter bearers'. In the town square, De Soto dismounted and walked to the low mound where the cacique's house stood. De Soto peered into the unoccupied house and then looked nervously at the long rows of empty huts. "Where are the people?"

At that moment, drums sounded, and a procession of Chickasaws entered the town. At the head, on a litter, rode the chief draped in robes of white skins. Surrounding him were fifty or more attendants, baskets strapped to their backs. The procession stopped in front of De Soto. At a signal from the chief, the baskets were emptied at De Soto's feet. Out poured woven straw blankets, furs, meat, fish, corn, beans. The Chickasaws have been watching closely for a long time, Cochula thought, to know how desperately De Soto needs supplies.

The chief bowed to De Soto and said, "I am Halloka, chief of the Chickasaws. My people have heard of your coming for a long time. All that we have is yours. The town is yours alone." Then the chief presented De Soto with a buffalo robe. De Soto drew it around his shivering body and bowed so low to Halloka that Cochula feared he would fall on his face.

The next day De Soto prepared a feast for Halloka and his head warriors. The Chickasaws would be treated to a delicacy they had never tasted—roasted pig.

All day the fattest swine were turned on the spit until the whole camp smelled of the succulent meat.

De Soto wants this chief to stay friendly, Cochula thought. That is why he feeds him this tasty meat.

Cochula and Zia helped to round up the pigs for the slaughter. Zia joined in the chase with the other dogs who had learned to herd the pigs. Racing along, sometimes rolling over and upturned by a fleeing pig, Zia would get back on her long legs, shake herself, and reenter the chase. When she bumped against Jabato, he bared his teeth at the impact and growled. Zia's short ears fell back and her tail tucked at the rebuff; she sidled away from the pack and lay with her muzzle on her paws at Cochula's feet, watching.

Antonio had been handling the dogs during the roundup, but now he came to Cochula's side. He had seen Cochula and Zia only from a distance since the night Pedro had died. He did not look at Cochula now but bent down and cupped Zia's long, pointed head in his hand. He raised the dog's head and looked deep into her large eyes. He felt along her lithe body, examined the slender legs and small, strong feet, and ran his fingers the length of her sweeping tail.

"She is a true Galgo (greyhound), like her mother

Pepita," Antonio said. "But she must be trained."

"To kill my people." Cochula pulled her hood close around her face and turned away from Antonio.

"No. To be your companion and guard dog. My mother's greyhound saved her from a pack of wild dogs. And she was my nursemaid. She protected us."

Cochula turned and looked at Antonio, his blue eyes bright with memory of his family.

Then he said, "Bring her each day to me as you to go to search for your medicines. Zia will become a *perro sabio* (a learned dog)."

Zia followed Cochula back to De Soto's quarters, but she turned her head frequently to look back at Antonio.

That night Chickasaws and Spaniards feasted together. In the king's house De Soto entertained Halloka and his warriors, with Cochula at his side.

"You will be with me," De Soto had said. "Halloka will see that we honor royal persons."

When Cochula entered the room, Zia close to her, Halloka's eyes widened at the sight of the dog and he stepped back a pace. "The dog will not attack unless commanded," De Soto assured Halloka. "She is the guard dog of the Princess Cochula who travels with us."

Halloka nodded to acknowledge Cochula's presence. He does not seem like a fierce Chickasaw, Cochula thought. He is like Talemicco, with his feathered headdress and commanding air. But, unlike Talemicco, he wore a necklace of bear claws, not a gold disc.

"We have heard much of your dogs," said Halloka. He studied Zia, sitting on her haunches, ears pricked, eyes alertly fixed on the chief. He noted that Zia's collar and Cochula's headband matched in color. "Chickasaw dogs do not fight. Our enemies would flee before us if we had such dogs."

"We have no dogs to spare." De Soto smiled as he spoke. "But we do have swine."

He drew his sword and cut a slice of meat from the roasted pig. Halloka took the meat and ate it. He watched Zia's every move.

Cochula put her hand protectively on the dog's head. Her gaze did not flinch when Halloka turned to study her pitted face. He will see what this disease brought by the bearded invaders does to our people, she thought. Cochula hoped the chief would find a way to save the Chickasaw people. He was wise to empty the town for De Soto to occupy.

∞

The Spaniards settled into their winter quarters in Chicaza, the Chickasaw town. Halloka continued to be friendly, and De Soto rewarded him by marching on a town hostile to the chief and burning it.

Meantime, the chief and his head men had acquired a taste for roasted pig. De Soto put a double guard on the swine after too many pigs disappeared, to be roasted on Indian fires.

During the winter camp, tensions eased. The captains and the soldiers had come to accept Cochula and her young guard dog companion. They now called her by name and eagerly awaited her coming to treat their wounds and fevers.

Even the Indian women, who had attached themselves to the captains, providing food and comfort, treated Cochula with deference. Cochula accepted her role as a medicine woman. She did not think about escaping or returning to Coosa. But she would have liked to be with Antonio and the dogs, bringing up the rear, instead of leading the way with De Soto and the captains.

Cochula knew she was not really a medicine woman, not like Poosaneeka. Poosaneeka had believed in spiritual forces. Even now Cochula could hear her grandmother's chant as she called on the spirits in the healing ritual. "There are powerful spirits," Poosaneeka said. "These forces are everywhere, ready to warm us, to feed us, to heal us." With the drums pounding, the flutes playing, and Poosaneeka singing, Cochula could feel the power.

But without her own people, and held captive in a strange country, Cochula could not find the spirits. They must have died with Poosaneeka at Maubila.

Cochula ventured often into the surrounding countryside to gather herbs and plants, with Zia accompanying her. Under Antonio's tutelage, Zia had learned the basic commands and responded to Cochula's directions. Being a young dog, she liked to play, but she was learning to track and attack.

Cochula knew the Chickasaws followed her on these walks and that they would like to capture both her and the dog. She also knew she had a better chance of staying alive with the Spaniards than as a prisoner of the Chickasaws.

On one of her herb-gathering hunts Father Segura walked with her. She talked about gathering plants with her grandmother along the river banks around Coosa. Father Segura talked about ships with great sails that would someday take him back to Spain.

"You will be beautiful soon again, Cochula," he said as they searched for the red root of the willow. When they came to the stream where the willow grew, she dared to look at her reflection. Her face was no longer red and swollen, but it was still pitted.

"It is better," she said. Her eyes brightened and she smiled at the priest, who had never seen her smile before.

CHAPTER 8

In late March, 1541, De Soto gave orders to break the winter camp at Chicaza and prepare to move to the Great River. The Spaniards were well fed and clothed; the wounded had recovered. Cold winds no longer swept through the town. De Soto sent word to Chief Halloka to bring two hundred Chickasaws to serve as burden bearers for the food and clothing which the Chickasaws had provided. The chief replied that he would send the carriers the next day.

When Cochula heard this, she fastened Zia's collar around the dog's neck. She attached a leash to it.

"You must learn to be tethered." Zia sank her teeth into the lead and began to shake it furiously.

"No, this is not a game, Zia. You must learn to be tied."

Zia's ears shot up and her big amber eyes looked inquiringly into Cochula's face. Seeing Cochula's stern expression, the dog lay down at Cochula's feet.

Later Cochula sought out Antonio. She found him rounding up the swine, preparing for tomorrow's march. The dogs were tied, whining and barking, sensing the impending move.

"I do not think Halloka will bring two hundred of his own people to be De Soto's slaves." Cochula pulled her shawl close around her head and covered her mouth so only Antonio could hear her. "The Chickasaws want the horses and the pigs. I have seen them also watching the dogs."

Antonio looked around the square at the Spaniards busily preparing to march, eager to be off in their pursuit of gold. No Chickasaws were in sight. They had been friendly from the day De Soto occupied the town. Antonio saw nothing that would cause him to agree with Cochula.

"The Chickasaws are sly and treacherous." Cochula felt Antonio's doubt. "In Coosa we know the Chickasaws as ferocious fighters."

"What do you think they will do?" Antonio did not look at Cochula as he secured the collar around Jabato's neck.

"I do not know, but if you value the dogs, keep a close watch tonight."

She took Zia's leash and attached it to the dog's collar.

"Keep Zia with you." She handed the leash to Antonio. "The Chickasaw chief eyes her. She will be safer with you."

Zia had seen her mother, Pepita, and whined to be with her. Antonio loosed the dog, who made a running dive for Pepita. The dogs nuzzled each other. Then Zia crouched on her haunches and made a playful lunge at Pepita. The two rolled over and over until Pepita tired of the game. She rebuffed Zia with a soft growl.

Then Zia tried to imitate the deep bark of Jabato. "She has found her voice." Antonio laughed at the high-pitched bark of the half-grown dog. "I will keep her," he said.

"Perhaps when we get to the Great River," said

Antonio, looking at Cochula, "De Soto will free you and let you return to your people."

"Perhaps," Cochula replied. Her shawl hid most of her face from Antonio's searching gaze. Though still pitted, her skin was no longer scaly. As she walked away, Antonio thought she had more of the regal air he had first seen at Maubila.

Cochula slept lightly that night, missing Zia at her feet. She heard the distant *Who-hoo-hoo-hoo* of an owl and an answering hoot closer by. During the day the plaintive mews of a sapsucker had caused her to look up and wonder. The people of Coosa believed the sapsucker's call warned them of impending danger.

The Spaniards knew nothing of such warnings and slept soundly. Three hundred Chickasaw warriors slipped past the sleeping Spanish sentries just before dawn. Carrying small firepots, the Chickasaws started blazes in every part of the town.

The town was on fire before the Spaniards could

put on their doublets and britches or pick up their arms. The Chickasaws spared nothing. They set fire to the brush shelter where the horses were stabled and the enclosure where the pigs had been rounded up.

The Spaniards ran for their lives. All they wanted was to escape the blazing houses. Even outside they were not safe. The Chickasaws shot arrows into their unprotected bodies as they fled. Some of the horses broke their halters to escape the flames and stampeded through the town.

De Soto, who always slept clothed, managed to rescue his own steed and ride to safety outside the gates.

Cochula heard the padded footsteps outside the house at the same time that the sides and roof of thatch burst into flame. Instantly she felt heat from the crackling fire and saw smoke curling toward her. She put her hand over her mouth and nose and stumbled to Father Segura's bed. The priest sat upright, suddenly awakened, his eyes wide in terror. Already flames licked at his bed.

Cochula seized his arm, shouting, "Run, run,"

and dragged him out of the house, with no thought of clothing or sacraments or medicine.

When daylight came, Cochula made her way through the smoking ruins of the town to where the dogs were kept. The place was strangely silent. No barking, no whimpers. Cochula's heart lurched. Where was Zia? She covered her mouth with her hands to keep from crying out at the scene before her.

Antonio was moving from one charred body to another, calling the dogs by name. His face and clothing were blackened with soot. Cochula forced herself to go closer. She must know about Zia.

She touched Antonio lightly on the arm. He turned to face her, his eyes glazed in shock.

"Zia?" she asked, her voice quavering. The sound of her voice revived Antonio.

"I tied the dogs so the Chickasaws could not take them." Antonio looked at the still-smoldering posts where the dogs had been tied. "I could not get through the flames to free them. Pepita is dead."

Antonio buried his face in his hands and moaned. His whole body rocked with his agony. His words were like a knife in Cochula's heart. She was sure now Zia had been lost.

But again she whispered, "Zia?"

Antonio raised his head. "Jabato and Zia escaped. Jabato's strength enabled him to pull free; the chain held Zia too. They must have fled up the mountain. I will go after them."

Cochula quietly turned away and left Antonio with his grief. But her heart lifted. Zia was alive! "She will return to me," she said to herself over and over again as she made her way to help the Spaniards burned in the Chickasaw attack. Her medicine pouch had escaped the fire because she slept with it tied to her waist.

Later that day Antonio disappeared into the countryside in pursuit of the two remaining dogs. He had learned much about living off the land from the Indians in the two years the Spaniards had traveled through their land. He could use the bow and arrow, and a flintstone knife. He had learned about hunting and tracking. Clad in deerskin britches and a vest of bearskin, with a flint knife around his middle, he bore little resemblance to the Spanish lad who had left Spain three years before.

The surprise attack of the Chickasaws was more devastating to De Soto than the battle of Maubila. Fifty horses, about three hundred swine, and the dogs, except for Zia and Jabato, were lost in the fire. Twelve soldiers died and many suffered wounds and burns. Most of the Spaniards lost their clothing, their weapons, and their equipment. From now on they would clothe themselves as the Indians did—in skins and woven jackets. They salvaged the iron from the fire, set up a forge, and made new shields, swords, lances, and bridles for the horses. They did not make coats of mail; the joints in such coats had proved too vulnerable to Indian arrows.

CHAPTER 9

Antonio found a footpath up the mountain, one probably used by the Chickasaws in their attack. He moved cautiously, stopping at intervals to whistle for the dogs, but not shouting their names lest a Chickasaw hear him. Near the mountaintop, when night had overtaken him and he could no longer find the path, he took shelter under an overhanging rock. He lay down to rest, but he was too cold to sleep.

A rustling in the underbrush close by startled him, and he sat upright, peering into the darkness. Nothing. He lay down again after unsheathing his knife. Did he dare to light a fire? He remembered tales the Indian captives told of giant cougars who attacked lone hunters at night.

Quickly Antonio started a fire, a small one, feeding it with pine twigs and cones. Perhaps, he thought, the dogs will smell the fire and come. He settled down against the rock, facing the blackness beyond the shelter. As he studied the shadowy outlines of bushes and trees, he saw no movement but sensed he was being watched.

Slowly turning his head, he encountered the gaze of pairs of yellow eyes, reflecting the firelight. Antonio's heart bounded and he felt a tinge of fear up his spine, raising the hair on his neck. What animals watched him so stealthily? They could not, he reasoned, be cougars, or bears, who were lone predators. These animals were different. Then he remembered the howls in the night that had disturbed the dogs, Jabato especially. The dog had answered the howls with long, low, penetrating moans that seemed to come from some primeval past.

"You are wolves," Antonio whispered in awe. He raised a hand in salute. The circle of eyes disappeared noiselessly at his movement.

With daylight Antonio explored the cave behind the ledge, looking for signs of the dogs. When he found large droppings, he retreated, fearing the cougar, who, he knew, lived in caves. Once again he followed the footpath up the mountain, bolder now than he had been earlier. He called Jabato and Zia by name.

When he crested the mountain, he scaled a boulder to scan the landscape for any movement that might be dogs. What he saw set his heart racing: spread before him was an Indian town as large as Coosa. Mounds and a square and huts were surrounded by open fields; a river ran close by. The capital of the Chickasaws, he thought. This was the residence of the cacique who had visited De Soto.

Antonio fell flat on the rock, fearing Chickasaw scouts would spot him. As he lay watching, he heard the faint neighing of horses from below, and the even fainter bark of a dog. Indian dogs do not bark, he remembered.

Waiting until dark to descend the mountain, Antonio stayed close to the ground as he approached the Chickasaw town. He had blackened his face with soot and covered his head.

"If the dogs are here," he reasoned, "they will be with the cacique." He knew the chief's house would be in the plaza on a mound next to the temple mound. He also knew the Chickasaws were tracking De Soto's departure from their land, and they would not be expecting a lone Spaniard looking and acting like an Indian. Surprise must be at the heart of the rescue. He would hit and run, like the Chickasaws.

As he drew closer, Antonio heard low chants and a steady drumbeat. Assembled in the plaza, warriors circled a litter. Creeping between houses to get nearer, Antonio recognized Halloka. The chief bent over the litter and touched the figure on it.

"It is Jabato. They have captured him." Antonio fell closer to the ground. "They will torture me just as they do Jabato, if they find me."

But he could not move. He was paralyzed by what he saw. Halloka was rubbing ointment onto the dog's forepaws as the warriors danced and sang. Jabato raised his head weakly to snarl at the chief.

Antonio realized that the chief was treating Jabato's burns, probably with bear grease. And the dance led by the medicine man was part of the healing ritual. The Chickasaws must have found the dog unable to move. How far had he fled from the fire before collapsing? Would Chickasaw medicine save the life of Jabato?

And what of Zia, not so strong as Jabato? Had she survived?

Antonio wanted to bound from his hiding place so Jabato would know he was nearby. But he dared go no closer.

He did not hear the Chickasaw creeping up behind him. He felt the blunt end of a war club and crumpled unconscious to the ground.

When Antonio awoke, he lay with his hands bound on a mat in the chief's house. Halloka towered above him.

"The dog will not obey my commands," the chief said. "He bares his teeth and snaps at me. He does not know I am the chief."

Antonio blinked to clear his head. "I will teach him," he said, "but I cannot do it with my hands tied." Halloka looked down at the long-legged youth, his eyes raised boldly to meet the chief's gaze.

"How will you do that?" Halloka seated himself on a mat.

"I am Antonio, keeper and trainer of De Soto's dogs." Antonio hoped his voice sounded more sure than he felt. "Bring the dog. I will show you."

Jabato, able to walk but weak, was dragged into the room on a rope, all the strength of his massive body pulling against two Chickasaws at the other end of the rope. His head was covered with reed netting, like a hood, secured around his neck. They are smart to muzzle him, thought Antonio.

"My enemies know I have the great dog," said the chief. "They fear the dog more than fifty of my warriors. But I cannot do battle with them if he will not obey." Halloka approached the dog, who growled even though muzzled.

"Untie my hands and I will remove the hood," said Antonio. "He will not attack."

When Antonio's hands were untied, he took the rope from the Chickasaws and slowly approached the dog. "Jabato," he called softly. A whimper came from deep in the dog's chest and his tail began to beat the ground. Carefully Antonio eased the hood, freeing Jabato's head. Jabato threw himself with a great leap on Antonio, licking his face, almost knocking him to the ground. Antonio hugged the dog. "Good, Jabato, good dog."

Halloka watched this display, his eyes narrowed and suspicious. He signaled the guards to grasp the rope and pull the dog back. Feeling the pull on his neck, Jabato curled his lip and snarled.

"Stay," Antonio commanded. He loosened the rope around the dog's neck and stroked the hair pressed into the flesh.

"I am his master," he said to Halloka. "He will obey me."

"When will he obey me?" Halloka asked.

"Look him in the eye and speak to him softly."

To the Chickasaws, the Spanish dogs were mystical creatures, more like gods than animals. Halloka, who gave no thought to splitting open the skull of an enemy, hesitated to address the dog or to look at him directly.

Jabato sat on his haunches, his pink tongue lolling, content to be with Antonio.

"Jabato," Halloka's deep voice resounded, "I the chief of the Chickasaws greet you."

Jabato's ears came up, and he turned his head from side to side, watching Halloka closely as the chief inched closer.

"Halloka is our friend," whispered Antonio to the dog. At the word *friend*, Jabato raised a giant paw as if in greeting.

"Praise him," Antonio said to Halloka.

"Good dog, good dog." Halloka repeated the phrase. Jabato wagged his tail.

"That is enough for today." Halloka backed away. "If you try to escape with the dog or without the dog, you will be caught and stretched until you die. The women of the Chickasaw will have the pleasure of flaying your pale skin."

Antonio listened, but he believed he would find a way to escape with Jabato's help.

CHAPTER 10

The Spaniards, busy salvaging what they could from the fire, paid little attention to Cochula. On the second day after the fire, when Antonio and Zia did not return, Cochula began to drop bits of dried food into her medicine pouch.

Late on the third day, when Antonio still had not returned, she walked out of the camp into the woods, the pouch concealed under her dress. The sentry only nodded to her as she passed. He was trying to mend his burned doublet.

Cochula moved slowly among the low bushes, stopping to gather acorns. She waited until she was out of sight of the camp to take the path up the mountain. She did not think the dogs would have run far from the camp, unless in panic they had strayed from the path and now were lost roaming on the mountainside, unable to find a trail. Was Zia lying somewhere in the bushes, injured, defenseless against preying animals?

As she climbed, Cochula stopped frequently to look for signs of scuffling on the path, or brush pressed down on the sides. Out of hearing distance of the Spaniards, but still aware of Chickasaws nearby, she chanted in a rhythmic whisper, "Zia . . . Sister Dog . . . Jabato." The only answer was the shrill whistle of a hawk circling high overhead.

By nightfall, when she had found nothing, she was sure Antonio had been captured by the Chickasaws, and perhaps the dogs with him.

Cochula had been climbing steadily. The path was strewn with loose rocks which slid under her feet. Soon she had to pull herself up and over boulders, holding on to young trees in the crevices. Finally, above her, she saw a rock ledge protected by an overhanging cliff. She climbed on it and prepared for the night. "Tomorrow I will find them," she told herself.

Alone on the mountain, without Zia, the night filled with creature noises, Cochula shivered. She would like to run back down the mountain to the safety of the Spanish camp.

"One day at a time," Grandmother had said. Cochula reached into her medicine pouch and pulled out the shell gorget her grandmother had worn. Cochula traced the spider engraving; the shell was cool to her touch and calming. The spider was a heroine to Cochula's people. She had brought fire to the people when no other animal could, holding it in a *tusti* bowl. Cochula removed the cross Father Segura had given her for protection and thrust it deep into her pouch, out of sight. Then she slipped the leather-thonged pendant with its shell gorget over her head. She felt braver now. She would rest in the shelter of the overhang until day came.

Ow-oo-ow. Yi-e-e-e. It was a cool night, and the sound carried far in the crisp air. Cochula first heard the wolf howl far below her and then an answering call from just above her. The wolves are talking, Cochula said to herself. More voices joined in, and Cochula remembered wolves singing on the moun-tain above Coosa. "They sing when they are content and their howls tell us things," Grandmother said. "What kind of things?" Cochula had asked.

"Things we don't know."

Could the wolves tell her where Zia was? Maybe they were just telling her animals have their own way to communicate. Was there a way she could communicate with the lost dogs?

When daylight came, Cochula slipped the shawl from her shoulders and spread it on the ledge in a sheltered place. Antonio had said dogs know the smell of their masters. If Zia finds the path, she will follow my scent to the shawl. She will know I have been here and she will wait for me, she reasoned.

Cochula returned to the Spanish camp. Only Father Segura questioned her about her overnight absence. De Soto had not missed her.

Once again, late in the day after she had tended the sick, she slipped away from the camp and climbed the trail up the mountainside. This time she climbed faster, eager to reach the ledge. Was it possible Zia had found the shawl and would be there waiting?

She pulled herself up on the ledge, her heart pounding. She spotted the shawl. It was not as she had left it, but in a ball, flattened in the center like a nest. Zia was not there. At that moment she heard a whimper behind her. A wet nose nuzzled her hand.

"Sister Dog, my Sister Dog," Cochula whispered, hugging Zia to her. Zia licked her face. "You made a bed in my shawl. You knew I would come back. You are a smart dog!"

Zia's tail thumped wildly on the rock as she gazed at Cochula.

Cochula ran her hands over the dog's body, feeling the long slender legs, the arched neck and head. There were no burns, as Cochula had feared, but Zia's paws had suffered cuts and bruises from the rocks.

"You climbed to escape the Chickasaws! Did you hide in the cave?" Cochula dabbed a salve from her pouch onto Zia's paw as she talked. "But where is Jabato?"

As the sound of his name, Zia's ears came up and

she looked around her. "We will find him and Antonio." Cochula took dried strips of deer meat from her pouch and gave them to the hungry dog, while she ate berries.

Later, with Zia at her heels, Cochula started to climb down the rock from the cave onto the trail. It was then she heard a rock sliding on the path below her.

Ramos had seen Cochula leave camp on both days. He saw the basket strapped to her back and noticed it weighed her down. He also noticed she did not stop to pick berries the second day.

"She is not coming back," Ramos said to himself. "De Soto will miss his medicine woman." Ramos hobbled to the forge where the blacksmith was making lances from broken weapons melted down in the fire.

"Captain Valdez sent me to fetch him a lance," Ramos said to the blacksmith as he picked up a weapon. Slowly, because he was lame, Ramos started

up the mountain path, using the lance to pull himself
along.

∞

When Cochula heard the noise she stopped,
rooted to the ground. It is not a Chickasaw, she
thought. A Chickasaw would never betray himself
that way. She crawled back on the ledge as far as
possible, pulling Zia with her. The dog had picked up
a scent and her muzzle lifted and her nose twitched.
Cochula clamped her fingers around the dog's muzzle
so she would not bark and held her pressed against
her body.

Cochula saw the point of the lance before she
saw Ramos. He had seen the cave; he stumbled over
the rocks toward it, careful to keep the lance pointed
straight ahead.

"Cochula, medicine lady," he called. "Come
down to Ramos."

Cochula pushed back into the cave's entrance.
She could feel Zia's body quivering. A low growl was
building up in the dog's chest.

"Little Indian dogs make tasty eating." Ramos was carefully picking his way among the rocks, using the lance to help him get to the ledge. He raised his voice to be sure Cochula heard him: "But not so good as the long shank of a regal dog of war."

At those words, Cochula felt a savage fury. She flung her head back. "He will not have you," she said, tightening her hold on Zia.

She was far back into the cave entrance now. She could see Ramos peering in.

"I will wait, medicine lady." Ramos laughed and settled down against a boulder on the ledge, the lance pointing into the cave.

Cochula knew the caves above Coosa where her ancestors hid from their enemies. She remembered Utina had escaped from the cave when he found a second way out. But without a torch how was she to find another way out in the dank and chilly darkness of this cave? Cochula felt Zia pressing against her, tense, waiting to obey her command.

Cochula had seen the dogs training under Antonio's direction. Zia had followed the pack, sniffing the ground, baying at the scents, learning to be a dog of war.

Was she ready?

Cochula remembered Ramos's skill as a lancer. But, she thought, even Ramos with his lance is no match for an attacking dog. She felt along the cave floor until she found a rock as big as her fist. She hurled it out of the cave, not at Ramos but down the mountainside. Startled, Ramos leaned to peer down the path.

"Attack!" Cochula commanded Zia, as she released the dog. Zia covered the distance to Ramos in two bounding leaps. The impact sent Ramos toppling over the cliff, his lance clattering down the mountainside. Zia was instantly on top of him, her teeth ready to sink into his throat.

Cochula looked down on the helpless Spaniard. She remembered the command Antonio had given, recalling Buteo as he attacked the Indian in Coosa. If Zia killed now, she would be a blooded hound, eager to pursue and kill again. The path of De Soto was marked with the bodies of her people who had been thrown to the dogs. Now she, daughter of the chief of Coosa, was about to condemn a Spaniard to the same fate.

"Come back!" she shouted to the dog below. Zia fell back and bounded up to Cochula, tail high. Ramos lay where he had fallen, too frightened to move.

"Go, Ramos," she said, in a tone used for the swine.

∞

As Cochula continued her search up the mountain for signs of Antonio and Jabato, Ramos limped back to the camp. He hailed Captain Valdez and demanded to speak to De Soto.

"The Adelantado has no time for such as you." Valdez spurred his horse and started to ride off.

"He will when I tell him his medicine lady has escaped."

Valdez reined in his horse and looked down at Ramos.

"How do you know this?"

"I followed her up the mountain. She tried to kill me."

"I will take you to De Soto."

After De Soto heard Ramos's story, he sent two captains, mounted on the strongest horses, in pursuit of Cochula. They caught her on the trail almost at the crest of the mountain. Cochula did not resist the iron collar they put around her neck. The captains granted her request that she be allowed to put the chain around the dog's neck. They feared to do otherwise.

When Cochula was brought to De Soto, he wasted few words.

"Ramos said you tried to kill him."

"He lies. He wanted to kill the dog and take revenge on me for his lameness."

De Soto fingered his beard and studied Cochula, noting the fire in her eyes. *She no longer hides her face in shame*, he thought. *In spite of the pockmarks on her bronzed skin, she is proud—proud as the Queen of Spain, and as difficult.*

He circled Cochula slowly as he spoke. "Tomorrow we begin our march to the Great River. On the other side, says your brother Utina, is gold.

"I will not have my way slowed by escaping Indians."

As he spoke, De Soto stood behind Cochula and wound his fingers into her short hair. Then he spun her around to face him. Cochula endured the pain, her teeth clenched. Zia bared her teeth, straining at the chain.

"If you try to escape again, I will kill you slowly like the Indians kill, in bits and pieces. The dog will come with me."

De Soto fixed his dark gaze on Zia.

"Leave the shackles on the dog," he commanded Valdez. "Free the girl."

Cochula's voice was low, almost a hiss: "If you take the dog, I will not be your medicine woman; I will not help you reach the river."

De Soto beat his fists together and circled Cochula in long strides. He narrowed his eyes until they were mere slits. Finally he replied, "Keep the dog. I have no time for such trifles."

Cochula made no more attempts to escape. Sometimes at night, lying on her mat, she dreamed of finding Antonio and of returning to Coosa. But she recalled the hardness of the iron collar around her neck and Zia's painful cry when Captain Valdez kicked his boot into the dog's side. So when morning came, Cochula gathered her medicines and prepared for another day of being a medicine woman.

PART III

To the Great River
April 25 to June 19, 1541

CHAPTER 11

On April 25, 1541, De Soto ordered his captains to break camp and move west out of Chickasaw country. The army had spent two months recovering from the Chickasaw attack. Most of the soldiers were now bareheaded and barefooted, clothed in shirts made from woven cane taken from the Indians.

The captains reminded De Soto that their food supply was low and there were many sick and wounded who had to be carried. "We will find a friendly cacique," De Soto assured the captains, "when we leave Chickasaw country."

No friendly Indians appeared to welcome the Spaniards to their chiefdoms. And there were no towns to occupy and pillage. But Cochula knew that Indians lurked along the trail, stealthily waiting a chance to attack. She knew the Indians would like to capture her and Zia, so she stayed close to the main force.

De Soto's desperation increased each day, as the corn from the Chickasaws was consumed and the men began to dig roots for food.

De Soto summoned Cochula. She saw that the Spaniard's eyes were glazed and hollow-looking. "Utina, your brother, did not tell me the straight way. We will all die before we reach the Great River.

"You are a medicine woman with strange powers. Our priests summon us to morning prayers and evening vespers. But they do not find food and clothing. Find us a friendly cacique."

Cochula met De Soto's burning gaze with a calm look. "I do not know the way to the Great River, the Chucagua. Your captains must find the way."

"But they are lost. We are in a wilderness." De Soto's voice was thin and high.

A wilderness with an Indian behind every bush, Cochula thought. These Indians would put an end to bearded invaders. They know the Spaniards are desperate for food.

Cochula found that in treating them for their wounds and illnesses she had come to care whether the Spaniards lived or died. They were not her people, but they were Antonio's people. And she believed he would return.

Did her own people, the people of Coosa, still exist? She did not know. But she found she wanted to live—for Zia, for Antonio, for herself.

To De Soto she replied, "This is not a wilderness. The people hide from you because you pretend friendliness and then enslave us. If we greet you in friendship you still enslave us."

Cochula's reply so angered De Soto that he stomped his feet and threatened to put the iron collar around her neck again. Instead, he ordered that she be mounted on a horse and ride by his side at all times. He hoped that Indians observing them would hesitate to attack.

Cochula did not like being on the horse's back, but from that position she could see the land better. Every day she scanned the horizon for the sight of Antonio and Jabato. All she saw was Ramos, limping along with the swine, now a small herd of fewer than one hundred animals.

❧

The bond between Cochula and Zia grew. The dog was her constant companion and protector as De Soto pushed to the Great River.

Zia had matured into a regal beauty. She had the marks of a true Spanish greyhound: a long, arching neck and pointed muzzle and head.

Now that Zia was fully grown, Cochula sensed a change in her. The dog was restless. At night Cochula was aware of Zia, bedded down at her feet, tense, turning, listening. She hears the wolves, Cochula thought. She wants to run with the pack.

At such times, Cochula reached down, stroking the dog to quiet her. "Sister Dog, Sister Dog."

The wolf pack appeared to be following the expedition, keeping pace in the wooded hills. Cochula listened to their howls. The howls are not all the same—like our voices are different, she thought.

There always seemed to be a lone howler, a wolf

by himself, away from the pack. Zia listened too. Sometimes she sat on her haunches and howled back.

One cool night Cochula lay close to a campfire, Zia at her side. As her eyelids flickered sleepily, just beyond the fire Cochula saw a movement, a reddish flash. She lay still, feeling Zia's body grow alert at her side. Once again the flash, and Cochula glimpsed yellow eyes and long, sharp ears. She knew it was a wolf, the loner. Zia sat up, ears forward, head raised, sniffing the air. Then, Zia disappeared beyond the fire into the dark. Cochula made no attempt to stop her. She knew Zia was ready to mate.

The next day Cochula slowly prepared the medicine baskets for the day's journey. She believed Zia would return, but she was reluctant to leave the campsite. De Soto dispatched Captain Valdez to check on his medicine woman, sending with him a horse on which to bring her back.

"Where is the dog?" Valdez asked when he saw Cochula alone.

"She went hunting." Cochula busied herself with her herbs.

"De Soto wants you now."

The sun was directly overhead when Cochula, riding with Father Segura, was aware of barking behind her. She turned in the saddle to see Zia racing toward her. Cochula dismounted hurriedly and embraced the dog. "Sister Dog, Sister Dog," she whispered.

To Father Segura's puzzlement, Cochula suddenly threw back her head, cupped her hands around her mouth, and imitated the howl of a wolf. Zia's lip curled in what Cochula knew was a smile.

Late in a day's march, the Spaniards came upon the Indian town of Quizquiz. Only women and children came out to greet De Soto. When he discovered the men of the town were away engaged in battle with the warriors of another town, he put the women and children in chains, holding them hostage.

When the warriors returned, De Soto agreed to release the hostages if the cacique of Quizquiz would supply a guide to the Great River and assure the

Spaniards safe passage through the land. The cacique agreed and gave De Soto a native guide.

On the next day's march Cochula rode behind De Soto with Zia on a lead at her side. When the guide turned from the main trail into a swampy area of tall grasses, Cochula asked Captain Rodriguez, "Where are we going?"

"The guide knows a short way," Rodriguez said.

Soon the horses were backing up as the ground became soggy, pulling their feet out of the mud with great popping noises. Cochula dismounted when her horse balked at slogging through the high grass. She had to lead the horse through the mire, holding on to Zia's lead at the same time. Zia whined, her long, delicate legs ill suited to plodding through mud. The dog tried to leap out of the bog, only to fall back.

"There is higher ground ahead," Rodriguez shouted back.

The high ground got the horses out of the muck, but the ground was no more than small islands of matted grasses and mud. The ground quivered when the horses moved. The animals neighed, their heads rearing up, eyes rolling in fear. Zia pressed against Cochula, shivering.

Cochula looked around her for help. All she could see were tangled masses of undergrowth and giant oaks blocking the sky. It was dark, dank, and eerie. Ahead she saw De Soto stand in his stirrups, desperately peering right and left.

The Indian guide, a pole in his hand, appeared to be testing the ground ahead for De Soto to ride over. Cochula saw, however, that when an opening appeared in the dense undergrowth, the guide turned away from it and moved down another dark, shallow waterway, beckoning the horsemen to follow. Soon the army was winding like a snake, deeper and deeper into the swamp.

Cochula followed in the line of march, but she knew the chief of Quizquiz, who had appeared to be friendly, had instructed the guide to lose the Spaniards in the swamp. There they would perish, unable to find a way out. The Indians would be rid of the invaders at last.

The first night in the swamp, Cochula lay propped

up on her saddle, Zia curled close to her. The medicine pouch was at her feet. She heard groans of weary and sick soldiers. Nervous horses stomped and snorted. At a distance an owl called and another answered. A rustling in the bushes alerted Cochula. She sat up; Zia growled. By the moonlight filtering through the trees Cochula watched an opossum waddling away. She drew Zia close to her.

The next day De Soto skillfully slashed the guide's left ear from his head and threatened to remove the other ear if he did not lead the army out of the swamp. The guide pressed his hand to his ear and bowed low to let De Soto know he understood.

Cochula cracked walnuts she had gathered earlier, dug potato roots, and shared her food with the dog and the horse. She was on her knees mending her horse's saddle when her eye fell on a piece of broken pottery. She picked it up and saw an incised pattern, a duck head of the same design used in Coosa. "The People, my people, have cooked here," she said to herself.

She dropped to her knees to look for more

pottery, but De Soto had given the order to move. She put the fragment into her pouch.

All that day the army wandered. The cavalry met itself returning, having moved in circles. By noon of the next day De Soto had removed the guide's other ear. "I would feed you to the dogs," he hissed, "if the devil Chickasaws had not burned them."

Then he blinked his eyes. "Aha!" he cried.

"But we do have a dog. A greyhound."

De Soto turned to Valdez. "Bring Cochula and the dog."

When the Indian saw Zia, he fell on his face moaning, holding his bleeding head.

Zia stood regally by Cochula, alert but unconcerned.

"This red-skinned devil has led us into hell," De Soto raged. "Loose the dog on him. At least she can eat."

"Sit," Cochula commanded Zia. To De Soto she said, "We are all lost without a guide."

She stepped forward past De Soto, pulled a bandage from her pouch, and wound it tightly around the Indian's bleeding head. "Give him a horse to escape on," she said. "Zia and I will follow."

"Is this another Indian trick?" De Soto said.

"He will lead us out," Cochula replied.

A horse, not saddled but bridled, was brought, and De Soto gestured to the guide to mount and be off. Terror of the dog propelled the guide off the ground onto the horse's back. He kicked his heels into the horse's side. The horse bolted forward into a clearing. Zia was barking, sensing a chase.

"After him!" Cochula commanded Zia, removing the lead. The greyhound sprang forward, baying and yipping, in pursuit. Hearing the dog behind him, the Indian wasted no time. Behind Zia, Cochula rode, holding her horse back so Zia would not be distracted from the chase.

Ahead she saw the Indian rein the horse through brush and disappear into swampy water. Zia will lose the trail in water, she thought.

There was silence, then Zia's baying again. Cochula urged the horse on. She saw the Indian and his horse splashing. Zia was trying to follow along the edge without entering the water. The Indian made no attempt to get out of the water.

The splashing stopped. Zia was quiet. A horse neighed. Cochula came closer. The horse had been pulled out of the water and tied to a tree. Then she saw the Indian, poling a dugout canoe down the waterway, fast disappearing into the dark shadows. That's it! Cochula thought. The way out is a waterway.

A shallow canal had been dug by Indians to get through the swamp. The guide knew where it was and where the canoe was hidden. He had planned his escape. Cochula called to Zia, who loped back to her, having lost all interest in the chase.

Following her horse's track back to the Spaniards, Cochula remembered the pottery she had picked up. "The canal must have been dug in ancient times by the People to cross the swamp. The People have been here."

She found De Soto waiting impatiently. She told him the guide had escaped but that she had found a way out. His eyes brightened. "Tomorrow we move again to the Great River and the gold beyond."

Cochula lay awake that night. She wondered if the guide had returned safely to Quizquiz. She hoped she had bandaged his head tightly enough to stop the bleeding.

Her scheme to let the guide escape so the Spaniards could follow him out of the swamp had worked. Zia nuzzled her hand. Cochula felt content. Looking up through the trees she could see the sky dappled with stars.

"I will tell you a story, Zia, about the heavens.

"Once, long, long ago, a hunter lived up in the sky. The pouch of cornmeal he carried was stolen from him by a white dog.

"As the dog ran across the sky, the pouch came open. The cornmeal was scattered in a broad white trail across the heavens. From that day the trail has been known as the White Dog's Road (the Milky Way)."

CHAPTER 12

It was May, 1541, when Cochula first glimpsed the Great River. She stood on top of the temple mound of an abandoned town De Soto had occupied. He had ordered Cochula and Father Segura to climb the high mound with him, to look for the river. When he saw it, he sucked in his breath.

"It is the Rio Grande, the king of rivers," he said.

To Cochula the river seemed as wide as the sky. "The Chucagua," she whispered in awe. It is like a giant monster, she thought, slithering around bends, rising and falling softly. Across the river, to the west, she could make out moving figures silhouetted on the horizon.

She turned and looked toward the east, toward Coosa. If I cross this river, she thought, I will leave my people behind forever.

And Antonio, where is he? Had the Chickasaws

found him and meted out their usual punishment to captives?

As Cochula looked back on the way they had come, Father Segura studied the Indian young woman. Pox marks were still visible, but she had regained her proud air. Her black hair had grown to cover her ears. To Father Segura she seemed to have become even more a princess of her people.

Cochula turned to De Soto. "This is the Great River promised to you by my brother. On the other side are the mountains of gold."

De Soto looked at Cochula. "The princess of Coosa has proved to be of great worth to my captains and my men—and to me." Cochula remembered De Soto's promise to free the slave women of Coosa if they treated the wounded at Maubila. Only she had survived.

She fixed her gaze on a great heron circling a backwater pool. Her heart pounded in her chest. Was De Soto about to tell her she would be free, free to return to Coosa, free to find Antonio and Jabato?

For one month the Spaniards prepared to cross the river. They felled trees, melted down their weapons to make nails, and built four barges on which to cross.

As they worked, Indians from across the river harassed them. Each day a flotilla of over two hundred canoes appeared. The chief rode in a giant canoe with a deerskin canopy over him. Sixteen warriors paddled each canoe. The Indians' faces and bodies were brightly painted—red eyes, blue mouths; and their feathered headdresses fluttered as they paddled. Fortunately for the Spaniards, most of the arrows shot from the canoes were well out of range.

Cochula knew these fierce-looking warriors hoped to stop De Soto from crossing the river. She also knew their plan would fail.

"This must be a very rich cacique, who has much to hide," De Soto said to the captains. "Perhaps he will be the one to lead us to the gold."

Early on the morning of June 19, the loading of

the barges started. De Soto had instructed Cochula to help with the sick. They, with the swine, would cross the river first. Cochula tied Zia near the horses while she helped with the loading. She was to cross on the last barge with De Soto and the captains with their horses. There had been no further harassment from Indians across the river after De Soto had soldiers fire several rounds from their firearms.

As the swine were herded onto a pen on a barge, Ramos came close to Cochula and leered. "You remember Ramos? Make my arm well, medicine lady," Ramos taunted her. He smells like the swine, Cochula thought. He dares to say that because Zia is tied. She backed away.

While the other barges were being loaded, Cochula climbed the mound from which she had first viewed the river and from which she could see a great distance. She scanned the road to the east for the sight of Antonio. Nothing was on the road, but she saw movement in the trees. "The people of this town are waiting to return," she said to herself.

She thought about the long journey back to

Coosa. First there would be Chickasaw country. Warriors would be lurking along the trail, showing no respect for the chief of Coosa's daughter. And there were rivers to be crossed.

With a sigh she entered the temple house atop the mound. Peering into the dark recesses, she saw a few overturned pots and baskets. She knew the people had taken their temple treasures with them when they fled.

A shaft of light through the doorway fell on a feather half hidden under a basket, drawing Cochula's eye to the spot. When she leaned to pick it up, it would not come. She righted the overturned basket and the rays of the sun caught the iridescence of turkey feathers.

Cochula exclaimed in delight, "It is a royal cloak." She shook the dust from it and carried it out to the sunlight.

Then she held it up with both hands as if showing it to the people below.

"Listen. Ha. I am Cochula, daughter of Talemicco, chief of all of Coosa. Ha.

"Listen. Ha. I am granddaughter of Poosaneeka, medicine woman of Coosa. Ha.

"I come from the Sun Land." Cochula bowed to the east.

She looked to see that no Spaniards were watching. They were busy with the loading of the barges.

Cochula put the cloak around her shoulders and danced in a wide circle, shuffling her feet and chanting a drum beat. Each time around the circle became smaller, until she stood in the center of it.

"Listen. Ha. Cochula of Coosa stands in the center of the world." She remembered that Poosaneeka led this women's dance in the ceremonial ground at Coosa.

She heard Zia barking and the horses neighing as they were loaded onto the barges. Slowly she removed the cloak and took it back into the hut, tucking it under a basket. Shading her eyes, she scanned one last time the road to the east. There was no sign of Antonio or Jabato.

Cochula descended the mound and made her way to the river. She untied Zia and led her toward the barge. The dog sensed Cochula's despair and her long, curved tail dragged the ground.

The horses reared and snorted, pulling against their lines. The captains struggled to lead them onto the barges. De Soto's stallion was led by two foot soldiers, with De Soto directing. The barge swayed just as the horse was pulled onto it. He missed his step and, pawing the air wildly, fell into the swirling waters. For one moment his head stayed above the water, his eyes wide with terror.

De Soto, still on land, shouted to the soldiers to hold on to the reins, but the strong current pulled the reins from their hands. The horse disappeared in the muddy, swirling waters. De Soto ran along the riverbank, frantically looking for the horse to come to the surface.

Just as the horse's head appeared above water, a figure further down the bank dived into the river and grabbed the reins of the horse. Both man and horse disappeared underwater but surfaced downstream. The man, pulling with both hands on the rein, eased the horse out of the current to the shallow river's edge. He quieted the horse and led him back to De Soto.

"You are a brave man," De Soto said. Cochula's heart lurched as she recognized Antonio, his fair hair hanging to his shoulders. His head covering had been swept away in the water.

"You are not an Indian," De Soto said.

With his tanned skin and his lithe body, naked to the waist, he could pass for an Indian except for his fair hair.

"You know me, Sire. I am Antonio, keeper of the dogs of war." Antonio's voice did not quaver. It was rich and resonant, not like the Antonio of Coosa.

"So the Chickasaws did not roast you at the stake. You deserted me after the fire."

"I went into the hills to find the dogs."

"And did you find them?"

"Only one, Sire."

"Where is the dog?"

"He is a *tustenegge* (warrior) of the Chickasaws."

"A warrior?" De Soto's eyes widened in disbelief.

"Halloka gave him this honor after he proved

himself in battle." Antonio saw no need to tell De Soto that Jabato would receive another honor. When Antonio had bade Jabato farewell, Halloka said, "When I die Jabato will be buried with me. We will travel to the spirit world together."

"And how did you escape?" De Soto asked Antonio.

"Halloka set me free after I taught him about the dog. He would have made me a warrior also, but I do not belong with the Chickasaws."

De Soto shrugged his shoulders. "You are a very foolish young man. But your Indian ways will be helpful now, as we seek gold across the river. We must cross the river before dark."

De Soto looked back to the east. "This is a cursed land. No gold. Only Indians." He looked at Cochula, holding Zia's lead. "Take the dog," he said to Antonio. "She is a good dog. Like Buteo in some ways."

Antonio said nothing. He wondered if De Soto knew Buteo had sired Zia.

De Soto turned to Cochula. "You are free to return to Coosa."

Then, with a twitch of his head upward, he added, "Or you may cross the river with Antonio and Zia. I need a medicine woman." Dismissing Cochula and Antonio, De Soto made his way to the barge for the last crossing.

Cochula, her fingers resting on Zia's head, gazed at De Soto's retreating figure. She could feel Antonio at her side.

"Zia lives," he said. Antonio bent down and rubbed Zia's head and neck and pressed her close to him. Then he became aware of her swollen stomach. He held the dog at arm's length so he could see her better. Zia, her head high, returned his stunned look with a steady gaze.

"She is going to have wolf pups." Cochula felt her pulse quicken as she shared the news with Antonio.

Antonio responded with a war whoop he had learned from the Chickasaws. He danced and stomped around Cochula and Zia, his blue eyes alight with excitement.

The Spaniards, eager to be off in their pursuit of

gold, paid little attention to the strange behavior of Antonio. He appeared to be as much Indian as Spanish now.

As Cochula felt Antonio brush by her in his wild dance, her mind raced with many thoughts. "Maybe I will cross the river after all. Maybe my future lies to the west with Antonio and Zia." There was no returning to Coosa.

"Wherever I go, I will be Cochula of Coosa. I carry my world with me." She had learned this as she danced on the mound.

Cochula fingered the shell gorget hanging around her neck. She could feel the deerskin pouch safely tied around her waist. "Maybe I will become a real medicine woman like Poosaneeka."

She put Zia's lead in Antonio's hand, and the three stepped on the barge together to cross the river.

It was June 19, 1541.

POSTSCRIPT

After crossing the Mississippi River, the De Soto expedition wandered in the area now known as Arkansas and Texas, endlessly attacked by native peoples. De Soto fell ill and died in 1542, never having found gold. His weary followers tried to reach Mexico overland, without success. They returned to the river, built boats, floated downriver, then across the Gulf of Mexico.

On September 10, 1543, three hundred and twenty-two Spaniards and one hundred Indians reached Tampico, Mexico.

In 1559, another Spanish explorer, Tristan De Luna, sailed from Mexico to found a Spanish colony in the Mobile area.

Historians report that De Luna brought a native woman of Coosa as his interpreter. The woman had been with the De Soto expedition from the time it left

Coosa until survivors reached Mexico. She, with a scouting party De Luna sent up the Alabama River, seeking food, reached Coosa June 10, 1560. The woman is identified as the sister of the cacique of Coosa.

Cochula would have been thirty-five years old in 1560.